THE DEMON'S QUEEN

DEAL WITH A DEMON

KATEE ROBERT

TRINKETS & TALES LLC

Dear Reader,

This feels a bit like the end of an era. I knew from the moment Azazel walked on the page in Court of the Vampire Queen, that he needed his own story. I hope you enjoy it!

♡ Katy

CONTENT NOTES

Tropes: Captor/Captive

Tags: demon bargains, midsized heroine, size difference, it's too big no for real, magical castle, sex worker heroine, the slightest whiff of Beauty and the Beast, Daddy/baby girl, I just want someone to CHOOSE ME, yes I lied and tricked you into signing a contract but I had reasons! Were those reasons good? MAYBE , magic sex balm makes everything better

CWs: stalking (not the hero), threat of abuse (not the hero), abuse in the form of neglect (historical, off-page), elements of self harm, violence, breeding, panic attack (on page)

CHAPTER 1

EVE

Seven missed messages. On my personal phone, the one I most certainly don't give out to anyone but a select few friends. It's not a number I recognize, which all but confirms my suspicion that one of my clients has decided to ignore the rules of our arrangement and try to go around Pope to get to me. Again. Pope goes above and beyond to vet the people they send my way, but despite them being damn near prophetic when it comes to bad apples, sometimes people slip through.

I stare at my notifications, exhaustion seeming to increase the force of gravity against my bones. I already know what I'll hear when I check the voicemail, but I make myself do it anyways.

"Ginger, why did you cancel on me? I—"

Fuck. It's Tanner. He's been one of mine for years now and has shown every evidence of being a relatively nice guy, if on the selfish side. He likes only the lightest of the girlfriend experience, preferring to play like we're sneaking away together. Not one of my favorites—even though I know Pope would

3

lecture me for getting attached enough to have favorites—but he's consistent and he tips absurdly well.

I delete the voicemail and click on the next one.

"Ginger, what the fuck? Answer the fucking phone. I swear to god—"

Delete.

"Baby, I'm sorry. I shouldn't have said that. Please—"

Delete.

I delete the last four without listening. I've heard enough. I type out a quick message to Pope.

> Tanner Lockeye has become an issue. He found my personal number and is making a nuisance of himself.

POPE

> Another one? That's unlucky, even by your standards.

> Can you not make jokes right now? I just lost one of my best-paying clients.

POPE

> Sorry, doll. I'll take care of it. He won't bother you anymore.

I barely breathe a sigh of relief when another text pops up.

POPE

> Assuming this means you're free tonight.
> Azazel is on the waitlist if you're up for it.

Even though I know better, I can't help the little fizz of excitement reading his name brings me. Azazel is my favorite client. He shouldn't be, because every sign points to him becoming a problem at some point, but to date, he hasn't done anything to overstep my very stringent rules. So I ignore the potential future problems because I enjoy my time with him.

And he tips even better than Tanner.

> Set it up. Let me know the time and place.

A few minutes later, Pope sends over the information, and I start the process of getting ready. It's a soothing ritual to set down Eve for the night and drape Ginger around me. It's a small distinction, but a necessary one. I pin my long blond hair into an updo so that Azazel can run his fingers through and send my pins flying. He likes that a lot. He also likes me in jewel tones, so I pull out a deep-purple dress that clings to my body and doesn't *quite* look like it's offering up my breasts, but it's a close thing. He's over six feet, so I pull on my highest heels. For makeup, I keep it subtle and sultry: a light smokey eye and lips a couple of shades darker than my natural pink.

I leave my apartment and take the elevator down to the ground floor. There's a small corridor here with a doorman ensuring no one comes in without permission. That and a few other security features increased the cost of my rent dramatically, but it's worth it. I take great pains to ensure my clients aren't aware of my real name or where I live, because of cases like Tanner, where they get confused about our "relationship."

The doorman on shift right now is Rahul, an older man with the sweetest smile and warm medium-brown skin. I found out last year that he's an artist. The way he paints the city is abstract and so lovely, it makes my heart ache. Rahul gifts me with that smile as I step out. "Going to be a late night, Miss Eve?"

"Yes, sir." I stop next to him as an understated black town car pulls up. "Keep the lights on for me?"

"I always do." He opens the car door for me. "I'm off at six, but Fred will be on shift after me. He's a good one, so he'll take care of you."

I don't like Fred nearly as much as Rahul, but I can't deny that he's good at his job. "Thank you." I sink into the back seat. "Have a good night, Rahul."

"You too, Miss Eve." He shuts the door, careful not to catch the hem of my dress in the process, and then we're speeding away from the curb toward the high-end hotel I always meet Azazel at.

His preferences vary, but tonight he requested we have a drink in the hotel bar before going up to the room. I don't mind in the least. He's a great conversationalist, and while he very carefully doesn't share much of his past—no more than I do—he has no end of stories to entertain with. I'm not certain if they're lies or the truth, but they makes for a pleasant time either way. And I don't particularly care whether he's lying; I'm not his girlfriend, for all that I offer a similar experience for the right price.

The hotel bar is crowded for a weekday, but that's fine. It will give me a chance to people watch before Azazel arrives. I find a high-top table in the corner and arrange my chair so I can see the entirety of the room.

In the fifteen minutes I wait, I pick up more than one person doing their best to covertly slide a wedding ring into their pocket before approaching a prospective one-night stand. There's a person on the opposite side of the bar who I'm nearly certain shares my profession. They watch me closely before realizing I'm not looking to pick up a new client here, then they lose interest. It's all deeply entertaining.

Until a familiar man walks through the door—and *not* the one I'm expecting.

"Shit."

Tanner cases the room in a single sweep and starts toward me. How the fuck did he know I was here? Finding my phone number is difficult but not impossible. Finding my location? That offers up a number of problems that I don't have time to deal with, because he's closing the distance between us. Fast.

I try to catch the bartender's eye, but he's busy flirting with an exasperated businessperson who may or may not be interested. No help there. I bypass my phone and go for my Taser. Even if I could get a text off to Pope, it won't make a difference. I *know* they have someone in the building because it's standard practice, but it will take them too long to get here.

Tanner reaches me in seconds. He's a tall white guy with the kind of good old boy looks that are a generic sort of handsome. Or they are usually. Right now, he's nearly purple with rage. "You cheating bitch."

"Tanner." I keep my voice low and even. De-escalating. "I didn't expect to see you."

"Because you cancelled on me!" He's yelling, not seeming to care in the least that he's making a scene. The bartender finally lifts his head and narrows his eyes. Too damn late.

"I have rules. You broke them." I am not going to apologize for holding the boundaries that keep me safe, but fuck if I like this kind of mess. Azazel will be here any moment, and the last thing I want is to force him to deal with this. "And I'm not your girlfriend, your partner, or your wife. You are my *client*."

"Whore!"

I roll my eyes. I can't help it. "Yes, yes, that's very original. Please leave before the nice bartender calls the police." Pope will do worse; they do *not* like people fucking with those under their protection.

"I'm not leaving without you." Then the fool lifts his clenched fist to strike me.

I have my Taser halfway to his balls when a hand appears and grabs his wrist. Tanner grunts with the slowed effort, though I can tell by his eyes that he's waiting for the moment he can try to hit me again. We both look over at the same time to see Azazel standing there as if he appeared out of thin air. Azazel's got a bored look on his face . . . until you get to his dark eyes. They're filled with so much rage, I panic and Taser Tanner

7

in the balls just to do something other than embarrass myself by cowering.

His legs give out and he collapses. Except he doesn't hit the floor, because Azazel still has a hold of his wrist. It leaves him dangling like a toddler throwing a fit. The absurd urge to laugh nearly overwhelms me. This *cannot* be happening.

I clear my throat. "Azazel. Lovely to see you." He doesn't respond, doesn't so much as glance at me, all his murderous rage narrowed entirely on Tanner. Fuck. If I don't do something —and fast—he may go straight from protecting me to an assault charge. Or murder, for that matter.

I shove my Taser into my purse and rise to press my hand on Azazel's chest. "Leave him. He's not worth it."

"I think you'd be surprised on how I measure that worth." But he releases Tanner. Azazel turns smoothly, putting himself between me and the other man, and presses his hand to the center of my back. "Let's go."

Relief makes me a little dizzy, but I manage to walk out of the bar with my head held high, ignoring Tanner's increasing volume of curses behind us. It's only when we reach the lobby that Azazel hesitates. "I know we had a night arranged, but if you're too rattled, I completely understand."

If only he knew. It takes so much more than a mess like this to rattle me. Tanner is proving to be a nightmare, but he's not the worst I've dealt with. I smile up at Azazel, and I don't even have to fake it. He's as beautiful as a model: sun-kissed skin, dark eyes, and stylishly cut dark hair. But it's more than that. He's courteous, he seems to listen, and he eats my pussy like he never needs to breathe. If the bed play gets a little possessive, that's a red flag I'm happy to ignore until I can't do so any longer, because everything else with him is pure pleasure.

"Ginger?"

I laugh a little. "Sorry, just a little off from that encounter. I'm sorry you had to deal with that." I slip my hand into the crook of his arm. "As long as *you're* not turned off, I'd love to still spend the night with you, Azazel."

He's already turning toward the elevator. "There's nothing related to you that could turn me off." But as we step into the elevator and the doors start to close, I catch him watching the space as if expecting a threat to burst through the shrinking gap. Before I can comment on it, he smiles down at me. "You look lovely."

"Thank you. You always do, and you know it."

He chuckles. "You can't blame me for trying to impress you." He slides his hand down my spine before stopping at the small of my back. Azazel never gropes, never fumbles a single step of the dance we engage in from the moment we meet to the morning when he sees me to the waiting car.

I have the whole mess with Tanner to deal with tomorrow, but I'm not about to let it distract me from the pleasure of Azazel's company. I press him back against the wall of the elevator as it ascends and stroke my hands down his chest. I stop at the band of his pants, and his hips jerk before he can get himself under control. There's no lie in the wicked smile I give him. "You never fail to impress me. I highly doubt tonight will be the exception."

There's a flash in his dark eyes, there and gone in a moment, and then he sweeps me out of the elevator and down the hall to the hotel room. Once we're inside, I don't care about the luxuriousness of the room, because he's here with me and I can almost feel his hands against my bare skin.

Azazel is a classy motherfucker. He wants me enough that he's practically ripping my clothes off with his gaze, but he walks to the table and the waiting bottle of wine there. "Let's have a drink, and then we can talk about what I want from you tonight."

CHAPTER 2

EVE

*A*zazel is big on seduction. He doesn't get into role-playing or the various kinky stuff that other clients favor. The man truly leans into the girlfriend experience.

So I know my role. I take a seat on the luxurious couch in the suite and allow him to bring an unopened bottle of wine. I never have more than one drink while working, a rule I also apply to my clients. Alcohol changes people in sometimes unexpected ways, and I have no desire to put myself in a dangerous position. Or a messy one. I don't have a particular drive for children, and taking care of drunk adult ones is a task I avoid whenever possible.

Azazel expertly pours two glasses of red wine before setting the bottle aside. He brings them both to the couch, but instead of sitting close, he carefully eases down into the other side. Since he's over six feet tall, he has no problem passing my glass to me. "I would like something different tonight."

I almost sigh before I catch myself. *Different* doesn't have to default to a red flag, but with how my luck is currently running, I don't like my odds of making it out tonight with Azazel still as my client.

Still, I smile at him. That's Future Me's problem. "What did you have in mind?"

He takes a sip of his wine, almost as if he's nervous. But that can't be it. I just watched him remove Tanner as a threat without the slightest bit of effort. What could *he* possibly be nervous about?

I slide a little closer to him and press my free hand to his chest. "No matter what it is, honey, I promise I won't think less of you for it. Just talk to me."

He takes another too-large sip of his wine. "I would like to . . . role-play."

I keep my features carefully schooled in interest. What kind of role-play is he asking for that makes him *this* jumpy? Yes, it's a new ask, but it's hardly taboo . . . "You know I'm happy to do whatever you like, as long as you talk me through it first."

"I want . . ." He finally looks at me, his brown eyes so dark that they're nearly black. "I would like you to sign a contract."

I blink. "A contract." My mind whirls, but no matter which angle I come at this from, I can't see what would make him act like this. Contracts for bedroom games have existed long before a certain franchise made them popular a decade ago. They can sweeten the spice, can lay out the terms in a way that makes everyone feel safe. With that said . . . "Not a legally binding one."

He huffs out a faint laugh. "It won't hold up in any court in the country."

Some of my nerves ease, but I haven't survived this long by being a complete fool. "I'd like to read it before agreeing."

"Of course." He reaches into his designer suit jacket and produces a surprisingly small stack of papers. "Take your time."

I sip my wine and then set the glass on the coffee table so I have both my hands free. He may say this contract isn't meant to hold up in court, but Pope would flog me bloody if I signed *anything* without reading it first.

It's three pages, hardly the densest reading, but detailed

enough that I have to go back to the beginning and parse through it more slowly. When I reach the end for the third time, I look at Azazel and arch my brows. "You want me to be yours for the rest of my life? Darling, I didn't know you had a marriage kink."

His smile is tighter than normal, his charm flickering in a way that truly does worry me. I hate to admit it, but this is one red flag too many. The best client may pretend that I'm theirs and theirs alone, but the moment our session ends, they don't fight the reality that this is just business. This contract may be pretend, but it represents a problem.

Worse, though, is the little warmth in my chest of *wanting*. I know better than to truly fall for my clients, though I'm human —I care for my favorites well beyond what they do for my bank account. They may fancy themselves in love with me, but they're in love with the fantasy of Ginger, with the experience I provide.

"It's a new development. Something I'm . . . trying out."

Understanding dawns, bringing with it an unforgivable sting. "This is a sample contract. You're going to do the real thing on some lucky partner?" I smack him lightly with the pages, trying to cover up my conflicted emotions with humor. "Why didn't you just say so?" I read through one last time. It's honestly thorough for how short it is. A lifetime commitment. An assurance that the safe word will be honored above all else. There's even a clause about what happens if children result from the union—something I will *not* be worrying about with my IUD and contractual use of protection with my partners.

Azazel, normally the very picture of cool and composed, actually blushes. "It's tacky."

I don't comment on that. "I'll sign this for the night if that's your fantasy. But I am curious about how you want to spend the rest of the time before dawn."

His eyes heat. "I have a few ideas."

I don't try to fight the pulse of pure need that goes through me in response to his lust. This, at least, is a known and acceptable emotion. I can fake it with the best of my peers, but Azazel is too damn perceptive. From the very first session, he read my body as if he possessed a map and set out to make me come as many times as possible before seeking his own completion. After the day I've had, a dozen orgasms sounds like just what the doctor ordered. Even so . . . "Indulge me and be specific."

He produces a pen and presses it into my palm. "I want to spoil you, Ginger. I want to treat you as if you were mine in truth."

"That's not specific." I wave the pen at him, even as my heart leaps. I know better than to believe pretty lies. Truly, I do. But sometimes the unloved orphan I spent my childhood being gets the best of me. Even though the world has proven itself cruel and selfish, in my heart of hearts, I simply want someone to choose *me*, to love me above all others. I'm too old for fairy tales —I have been since I was a child—but some fantasies persist even when you know better.

He grins almost ruefully. "Mostly, I want to shove up that dress and taste your cunt." He's achingly familiar like this, self-possessed and confident. "Once I get my fill, I'll fuck you. Again and again, until our time together is at an end."

I can't stop myself from squeezing my thighs together. "In that case . . ." I sign with a flourish.

It's not until I lift the pen that I realize my mistake. In my distraction, I haven't signed the name *Ginger*. Why would I? She's real only in these moments with my clients. I've never had to sign anything as her.

No, I sign it as *Eve*.

I press the papers to my chest. "I need a moment."

"It won't matter." Azazel drains his wine and sets the glass down on the table. "I'm sorry, Eve. You may never forgive me for this, but at least you'll be alive to hate me."

Fear slices through my lust, shredding it. "What did you say?" Even as I tell myself that I heard wrong, I know I haven't. He said *Eve.* My name. My *real* name. And it's not because he saw me scrawl it on the paper.

I stand abruptly. "I have to go. I'll issue you a full refund."

"It's too late for that." He still sounds regretful, which scares me more than anything else. I've ignored red flag after red flag, and now I'm in trouble I can't get myself out of. There will be no interruption to save me, not with a locked hotel door between me and the rest of the world. Damn it.

Azazel hasn't moved, so I take the opportunity to skirt the coffee table and dig my phone out of my purse. I shoot him a look, not sure if I should be more scared or less that he seems intent to let me do this.

Almost as if it really *doesn't* matter.

I don't bother texting Pope. I have to get the fuck out of here, and my hands are shaking so much, it's difficult to type out my passcode.

They pick up immediately. "What's wrong?" Of course they'd know something is wrong. I would never call them in the middle of a session without cause.

"I need an escort to the car." There's no need to get into the weirdness of this whole thing. Even as I think it, I'm struck by the fact that some fool part of my head is still sure Azazel won't hurt me. I don't know what the fuck is wrong with me. I've witnessed far too many instances where a "good" person turns feral and violent to those closest to them. Afterward, everyone wrings their hands and wonders how they didn't realize the danger.

In reality, the signs were there all along. They just chose to turn away from them. To continue in their happy little lives, sure that nothing bad could happen in *their* nice neighborhood. To believe that *this* client won't be the one who lashes out. I'm a fool.

Pope doesn't hesitate. "My man will be there in three minutes. Lock yourself in the bathroom if you need to. He has a key to the hotel room."

With anyone else, that would be a huge breach of trust. With Pope, it's the standard of doing business. They don't fuck around with their people's safety.

Azazel rises slowly to his feet, and I skitter back a few steps.

"Right. I'm going to do that." I hang up. There's no point in keeping Pope on the phone, and I'd prefer both my hands free if it comes to a fight.

He raises his hands, palms out. "I'm not going to hurt you, Eve."

"Stop saying that name." I edge back a few more steps. I know the layout of this suite well enough. The bathroom is just down the hall and to the left. Azazel is obviously strong, but surely not even he can break down a door in three minutes? Or two minutes now.

"Please calm down."

"No one in the history of the universe has ever calmed down when someone said to calm down." I back up another few steps. "Please don't come any closer. Pope's man is liable to shoot you."

"I didn't want things to go like this. I wanted to find another way." He drags a hand through his dark hair. "I'm sorry."

Now it's my turn to hold up my hands. I'm well into the hallway now, only about ten feet from the bathroom. "There's nothing to apologize for. Just . . . stay there."

"E—" He cuts himself off and sighs. "You're in danger."

"No shit." The words come out too high and tight. Despite my best efforts, my fear leaks in through the cracks. "Please don't come any closer."

"I'm not going to hurt you. I would never hurt you." He glances at the door, and his expression goes stony. "One day, you'll understand and forgive me for this."

Between one blink and the next, he's before me. I can't stop the scream that tears from my lungs as he wraps an arm around my back and hauls me against his chest. It doesn't hurt, but *no one* moves that fast. It's almost like he teleported. "I'm sorry."

"Please . . ." The room fades out around me. For a moment, I'm sure he drugged me, but my head feels clear despite the fear shrieking at me that I'm in danger.

I shove against his chest, but there's nowhere to go. I hear the hotel room burst open as everything goes black.

CHAPTER 3

AZAZEL

"*W*hat have you done?"

I don't look up as I carefully lay Eve on the bed. The room is nearly identical to those of the other human women I've made contracts with in the last few days. It's not what I would have chosen for Eve if circumstances were different . . . but circumstances aren't different.

She won't wake up for some time yet. A blessing, I suppose, since there's going to be hell to pay once she realizes all the ways I've lied to her.

"Azazel."

I finally look at Ramanu. They're one of the best bargainers I have, and unlike so many others in my court, they're not afraid of me. They stand with their hands planted on their hips, and if they had eyes, no doubt they would be narrowed. Instead of the customary single set of horns most bargainers have, Ramanu has two. The second, smaller, set curves out from where their eye sockets would be.

That doesn't stop them from seeing far too much.

They frown. "Tell me this isn't the human you've been sneaking off to play with for years."

As leader of the bargainers—king, if I'm being honest—I've learned to lie, cheat, steal, and even kill in the pursuit of bettering my people's lives. But I don't lie to Ramanu now. "This is Eve."

She stirs a little when I say her name, and I can't help turning back to her. Gods, she's beautiful. Long blond hair, full lips, a soft body filled with curves that I've spent hours exploring.

"*Azazel,*" Ramanu hisses. "You're endangering the plans that have been so long in the making. The territory leaders will be here *tomorrow.* You need to be focused."

They're right, but that doesn't change the fact I had no choice. The alternative was too horrible to bear. "I have it under control." It takes more effort than I will ever admit to turn away from the bed and walk past Ramanu to the door.

They follow, nearly stepping on my heels in the process. "You have one more bargain to make. You're cutting it close. If any of the leaders think you're hiding a human from them, they're going to start asking questions—or thinking the others are subpar options."

Which would put the four remaining women in danger.

"That won't be a problem." I shake my head sharply. "Belladonna is primed to say yes."

"Again, that doesn't change the presence of your blonde."

I feel like I'm free-falling, but when has that stopped me from forward momentum? For peace in this realm, I've allowed myself to become a monster in so many ways. To hurt the one person I meant to keep separate. "Eve will participate in the auction."

"Of course. Why didn't I think of that?" Ramanu throws up their hands, their frustration coating the hallway. "You certainly won't go on a fucking rampage when someone else chooses her, unraveling all the work you've put in for peace in this realm."

They're doing what a good second-in-command does and

pointing out the flaws in my admittedly impulsive plan, but I still want to grab them by the throat and slam them into the wall. My predecessor would have; she ruled through terror as much as anything else. I've chosen a different path. Unfortunately, choosing a different path didn't banish the violent impulses I was forced to develop to stay alive in Caesarea's court.

My aunt was a monster. No one else was willing to step in to stop her, so the task fell to me.

"I will not do anything to endanger the auction, but I can't risk her presence causing questions, or anyone realizing how . . . special . . . she is to me."

Ramanu snorts. "And you give me grief for my fascination with that murderous little witch."

I start walking down the hall, and they fall into easy step next to me. "Your murderous little witch is a murderous *witch*. If you can secure a bargain with her, then she'll be an excellent addition to the court. But that's a rather large *if*, Ramanu."

They grin, quick and wicked. "I have my ways." Their smile fades far too quickly. "Why now, Azazel? You could have waited a week and the rest of them would've been too busy with their new humans to wonder what you're up to. You're a bargainer; of course you'd continue making deals."

I push open the massive wooden door at the end of the hallway and hold it for them. "The situation with my cousin has escalated. I got word today that he's aware of her."

Ramanu curses under their breath. "That's unfortunate."

"So you see, I didn't have a choice." In another week on her own, Eve would've been dead.

* * *

EVE

I wake up in an instant but keep my eyes closed as I listen to Azazel talk to someone with a light and melodious voice . . . Ramanu. It's sheer habit to keep my body relaxed and my breathing even. My mind, though? It's racing. The bed I'm lying on is unfamiliar. I can't hear Azazel's footsteps, so the room must have carpet instead of the marble floors of the hotel suite. More than that, the very air feels different. It takes several slow inhales before I fully register the . . . I don't know how to explain it. Hotel air has a definitive feel, sterile and a little off from a home. The air isn't humid, but I can't feel it actively leeching the moisture from my skin. And there's a faint scent in the air, something layered in the way of old houses. This is a room that's been *lived* in.

It adds up to one horrifying realization: That motherfucker kidnapped me.

I can barely register their words, can barely think past the screaming in my head. It's everything I can do to lie there and pretend to still be unconscious as Azazel and the other person leave and close the door softly behind them. Even then, I make myself count to one hundred slowly to ensure they're gone.

No one returns in the intervening time, so I slowly open my eyes with the intention of scanning my room for cameras—and a way out.

I lie on a massive four-poster bed, each post thick dark wood with carvings winding up its height. The comforter is thick and looks handmade. I drift my fingers over its surface, hating that I find the texture pleasing.

There's no point in playing possum any longer. I sit up slowly and take in the rest of the space. A large wardrobe hunches in the corner, big enough to hide three bodies. A doorway leads into what appears to be a bathroom. The door

Azazel left through is massive, easily eight feet tall and twice the width of normal doors.

And there's a window.

That gets me moving. If I can escape, I can flee and try to find a gas station or maybe another house close by and beg a phone call. No matter where Azazel's taken me, Pope will retrieve me. They'll come up with a plan that will see me home and safe. I just need to get out.

I rush to the window—an ornate curved thing that looks like it belongs in a castle—and freeze.

There's no glass, which should have been my first clue that something is wrong. The second is that we're not on the ground floor. In fact, we're so high up that I can see the entire city sprawled out at the base of my tower.

A city I've never seen before.

"No, no, don't panic. There are plenty of places in the world you haven't visited. This is just . . ." There are mountains in the distance, the massive peaks a deep blue-purple that hardly looks real. But that's not what has panic threatening to short out my thoughts.

No, that dubious privilege goes to the creature flying through the bright-blue sky in the distance. I almost convince myself it's some kind of predatory bird, but as it swoops down and then up again, appearing to ride the air currents, I have to admit what I'm seeing.

A person with crimson skin and large bat-like wings.

A fucking monster.

"This is not happening." Speaking aloud doesn't snap me out of the vision I'm trapped in. The creature in the distance continues to fly and spin, as graceful as any predatory bird I've ever seen. "Drugs. It has to be drugs."

But I don't feel high. I've dabbled in more than my fair share of mind-altering substances in my ill-spent youth, and there's a distinct feel to each of them. For a drug to make me hallucinate *this*, I should be feeling some other effects. I'm not.

A second monster joins the first, though this one appears to have a specific destination in mind, rather than the pure entertainment of being in the air. I rub my eyes—hard—but nothing changes when the dancing spots clear. "Maybe I'm having a nervous breakdown. Something snapped." Except my mind feels fine. I'm scared. I'm angry. I'm one sharp breath from panicking. All those sensations are familiar to me, even if this situation is far more dire than any I've encountered to date.

Someone knocks on my door, light and polite but also clearly not intending to be ignored. I sigh. "I don't know why you're knocking. It's not like I can say no."

The monster that emerges through the door is like nothing I've ever seen or imagined. Humanoid for the most part, but with the same deep-crimson skin as the flying one I just saw. It's their face that stops me short. They have two sets of horns, one seeming to replace where humans have eyes.

What the fuck?

"I'm Ramanu. They/them." They step into the room and close the door. They're wearing a black tunic-type garment that reaches their midthighs and little else aside from black sandals that lace up their muscular calves. "I'm sure you have questions."

Only half a million. I don't know whether to treat this as if it's all normal and fine or start screaming and never stop. "What did Azazel drug me with?"

They lean against the door and cross their arms over their chest. "No drugs. No hallucinations. Your mind hasn't broken. Azazel brought you to the demon realm."

"Of course. I'm not drugged or losing my mind; I'm in hell." I choke out a laugh. "Why didn't I think of that?"

"Not that Christian self-recrimination circle jerk." They wave that away. "I realize this is a lot for a nonmagical human to process, but there are countless realms in existence. Once upon a time, they were cozy and close." They press their palms together. "But a millenium ago, some kind of catastrophic event happened to scatter them." They yank their hands violently apart. "These days, unless you go through Threshold—which I don't recommend— only a handful of beings can traverse realms. Like the bargainers." They point one clawed finger at themself. "My people have a long and storied history of coming to your realm and making bargains."

It's too much to process. This is impossible. It *should* be impossible. I close my eyes and force myself to just . . . accept. I can keep screaming internally that this is all the trick of a traumatized brain, but in the event it's not, I'll be at even more of a disadvantage if I keep resisting the truth that's right in front of me.

Bargains.

I open my eyes. "Bargains as in contracts."

"Bargains as in contracts," Ramanu agrees. "I won't pretend I understand what drove Azazel to change his plans, but rest assured that you're safe. Even if he weren't essentially king, these days no one in this city would dare abuse or threaten a human. Bargains are sacred to our people. Humans are to be protected."

If I assume this is all real, then I need to start plotting. I press the heels of my hands to my eyes and try to *think*. Azazel had me sign a contract. If Ramanu is to be believed, that contract is the reason he was able to bring me here. To go home, I just need to do those steps in reverse. "How does one cancel a contract—or a bargain, I guess?"

Ramanu grins. "It would have to be mutually agreed upon."

Something that won't happen, given how much effort Azazel went through to trick me and bring me here. "Oh."

"Of course," they say silkily, "there are other ways. If the terms of the contract are violated—in your favor, of course—

then it's null and void. The bargainer will be forced to fulfill their side of the deal and return you to your realm."

My mind trips over their words. I read that contract fully. "There's nothing in there about him giving me something. And when would it even come into play? The terms were for a lifetime."

If I weren't watching Ramanu so closely, I would miss the way their jaw drops. They recover quickly but not quickly enough.

I narrow my eyes. "That's not standard procedure, then."

They push off the door and shift their hands to their hips, a flirty position that does nothing to mask the fact that they're fidgeting. "You must be tired."

"I'm really not." I watch them closely. A good part of my profession is reading people, and while Ramanu may not share all the features of a human, they're not doing a good job of masking their emotions right now. "Those terms are abnormal, aren't they?"

They clear their throat. "There will be an event tomorrow night that requires your attendance. Please avail yourself to the wardrobe." They reach back for the doorknob. "In the meantime, you should rest. Food will be brought to your room and cleared when you're finished with it."

They're going to leave before giving me any answers. I start to slide off the bed. "What kind of event?"

"An auction, though not a traditional one. It may seem frightening, but have no fear. Azazel won't allow anyone to touch you. You're safe here." Then they're gone and the door has closed softly behind them.

What the *fuck* just happened?

CHAPTER 4

AZAZEL

*T*oday has been in the making from the moment I took over leadership of the bargainer demons, wresting it away from Caesarea once and for all. My aunt was content to drive us to ruin for the sake of her entertainment and bloodlust. Our realm is too damn small to be embroiled in a constant state of war. Whole populations have been decimated in service to her ambition. Whole generations—mine, notably—bear the scars that only war can bring.

I've vowed to go a different way. One where peace reigns. One where bargainers don't have the market cornered on power. It's been too many generations since humans and the people of this realm mingled freely. In a world where each territory takes its strength from the magic of its leader, everyone except us has been in a steady decline for far too long.

Just how Caesarea preferred it.

Today changes that, once and for all. I've worked exceedingly hard to create enough trust with the other territory leaders that they were willing to come here and accept my offer. And now it's happening.

Having Eve on the stage was never part of the plan.

I don't have a choice, though. Ramanu was right when they pointed out that any appearance of dishonesty will undermine the entire operation. Eve has to join the others, and I have to ensure no other leader chooses her. It's a mess of my own making, but even with the way time moves differently between realms, there was no guarantee that leaving Eve alone for another day wouldn't result in her death.

Brosh has spent a decade being a mere voice of discontent. I underestimated him, sure that he'd never escalate. To discover that not only had he found Eve, but he had plans to kill her? I shudder. I hadn't stopped to think. I needed her safe, and now she is. No matter what the cost ends up being, it's more than worth it as long as she remains among the living.

Still, there's the event to deal with. I do my best to focus as I pull Rusalka—the succubi and incubi leader—aside the moment they arrive and explain what I need from them. I'm concerned about one of the humans in the group tonight, and while I think we have the most peace-minded leaders in the realm possible, I'm not willing to sacrifice the human women on the altar of peace. There's a way forward for all of us; it just requires some careful maneuvering.

Once I have her agreement, it's time for the others. Thane from the krakens' territory. Bram from the gargoyles'. Sol, the dragon king. They're all smart people. They understand what I'm offering them immediately, even if they don't trust it entirely. That's fine. Better to ensure they take the offered truce with care.

The human women stand on a short dais in the front of the room, each in a different color of dress, watching us with wide eyes. Belladonna, Briar, Catalina, Grace . . . and Eve. I watch Eve's eyes go wider as she takes in Thane's tentacles, Bram's wings, Rusalka's hooves, and . . . Well, Sol. When her gaze lands on *me*, it's everything I can do to keep my expression composed as if I don't know her. She's never seen me in this form, and since she has plenty of cause to hate me currently, I thought it best to avoid a conversation until the rest of my business today is conducted.

I turn back to the leaders. "Let's begin."

Rusalka shifts forward, her eyes flaring crimson. "Red." Belladonna, just as we agreed upon previously.

I turn my attention to the others, waiting with my heart in my throat.

Bram rumbles a little, his wings flaring, but he finally shrugs as if fighting me even this much is too great an effort. "They're all the same to me. Purple."

Thank the gods. That was easier than I expected. "Very well." I force a sharp grin and turn to the two remaining leaders.

"Blue." Thane moves in his pool, tentacles shifting over one another beneath the water. The ones on his head—where the humans have hair—are mostly behaving, though there's a nod to his tension in the way they slither over his shoulders, moving in a wind that doesn't exist.

Now, there's only Sol remaining. The dragon considers me for a long moment, and I can practically see him weighing whether it's worth challenging me over the fact that he truly has no choice. "White." It's a good pairing. Sol is honorable to a fault, and Briar's soul is bruised from the abuse of her now-dead husband. He'll take great care with her, which is all I can ask for.

"Perfect." I clap my hands together, signaling for the light to go up. "Let's get these contracts taken care of."

It takes hours, despite everyone being eager to take their respective human and retreat to their territory. We have a good set of leaders in this generation. Even Thane and Bram, carrying so much loss that it threatens to crush them, are fair, if not kind. Sol is a teddy bear, as Ramanu is so fond of saying. Rusalka is a leader I respect deeply, and we already discussed my concerns over her human, Belladonna, not advocating for herself. There is no reason for the stress wrapping around my spine and threatening to crush me.

I am particular about who I offer contracts to. I have been even before becoming territory leader. Yes, a bargainer's power grows with each bargain signed and sealed, but offering one means taking responsibility for another person's well-being. Since becoming leader, I've only made one deal and it went badly. In the wake of that it was easier to make no deals at all. I had a whole territory to worry about, and adding more to my plate—even if resulted in more power—was too much to ask for.

Until now.

Creating five bargains and sending four of the humans involved off to live outside my domain and outside my control . . . I clench my fists. They'll be fine. According to the contracts each of the leaders signed, they will default their territories to me if their human is harmed.

If I thought any of the other leaders would be careless with their prizes, I never would have made this offer. I can't say they are all good matches, based on what I know of both the humans involved and the leaders, but hopefully things will fall out for the best.

As the last pair files out, heading for the portal that will transport them back to their home, I don't have an excuse for avoiding Eve any longer.

I sigh and head for her room, where she was escorted back after the others were chosen. I trail my hand along the stone wall. "Keep an eye on her, please. She's liable to get into trouble on her own."

The castle isn't technically sentient, but it's close enough, so it's a good idea to be polite and ask for what I want instead of demand it. Whichever leader in generations long past imbued the building with magic to shift and mold at will, I don't think they intended the place to end up with a will of its own. But magic and time have a way of playing with even the clearest of intent.

Case in point, it should be a five-minute walk to reach Eve's room. The castle must sense my reluctance, because it takes me fifteen to reach her door.

I pause. There's no avoiding this forever, and the longer I put it off, the worse it will be. I lied to her. I tricked her. And now I'm going to reveal myself to be a monster to her human eyes. I have enough magic that I *could* draw my human glamor around me, but it's difficult in this realm, and more importantly, it would only extend the lie.

I have her for a lifetime, and if she hates me for the entirety of it, at least she'll be alive to hate.

With one last aborted sigh, I knock firmly on the door. It cracks open immediately, the castle allowing me entry before Eve has a chance to decide for herself. When I don't immediately push the door open, it creaks wider on its own.

"Not helping," I mutter.

And then she's there, standing before me in her yellow dress, her dark eyes stony. "I'm overstimulated and not in the mood. Leave me alone."

"Eve."

It's agony to watch the expressions that play across her face. Shock, fear, uncertainty. She buttons it all up in seconds, but it's clear that she recognizes my voice, and it's equally clear that she doesn't know what to think of me in this form.

She clears her throat. "Azazel? I thought you sounded familiar in the other room, but . . ."

But I look nothing like the man she's known for years. "I'm sorry for how things occurred. You're safe here." Necessary words, for all that they feel inadequate.

She blinks, her uncertainty melting away to reveal pure rage. "You kidnapped me."

"You signed the contract." I register that it's the wrong thing to say immediately and hold up my hands. "I understand that—"

"I signed a contract you led me to believe was role-play!" She clenches her fists. "Did you kidnap the others too? Did you fuck them before they signed their lives away? And now you *sold* them. You're a monster." She flicks a derisive glance over my body, for all that I tower over her in my true form. "And it has nothing to do with how you look."

I flinch. I can't help it. "I haven't fucked anyone but you in years." I don't intend to speak that truth, but it lands in the space between us. I watch her discard my words as lies, and I have no one to blame but myself. Because I *did* lie to her.

Just not about this.

"Even if that were true, what do you want? A cookie?" With every word, she draws her composure tighter around herself, closing me out. "I am not, and never was, your girlfriend. You were a *client*."

It's the truth. There's no reason for it to sting. I'm no love-struck fool to think that she shares my feelings, no matter how much she seemed to enjoy our time together. I clear my throat. "And I didn't *sell* the others. The contracts were renegotiated."

"Renegotiated." She snorts. "Yeah. Sure. Whatever you say." She crosses her arms under her generous chest. "Are we done? Being in your presence is making me sick to my stomach."

I want to roar my frustration, but I haven't gotten to where I am today by letting my anger flare outward. Control is every-thing, and control is all I currently have to help me deal with Eve. I take a measured step back. "You're free to explore the castle as you like. No one here will harm you."

She narrows her eyes. "And if I want to leave?"

"You'll find the doors locked to you." I open my mouth to continue, to explain that it's not safe, even in this territory, that I have enemies who don't like the changes I've made, that those enemies are more than eager to take advantage of any perceived weakness, that *she* is my only perceived weakness . . .

But Eve slams the door in my face before I can get a word out.

I sigh. "Fuck."

* * *

EVE

I strip out of the yellow gown and dig through the wardrobe until I come up with clothing better suited to my needs. My mind still whirls with everything I've seen since yesterday. Monsters of every variety and yet still seeming so human seeming. Women handed over to them without a single hesitation. And . . . Azazel.

I pause, my hands on the buttons of my gown. He lied to me in so many ways. The contract, his history, even his appearance. Because the . . . being . . . who came to my door just now is the very same one who presided over the auction. He was tall as a human, but now he's got to be more than seven feet, and his shoulders explain why the doors here are so wide: any narrower and he'd have to go through them sideways. His skin is several shades darker than Ramanu's, and his horns are downright majestic, jutting from either side of his bald head and up. He's even handsome in a rough-cut way, though I'm not currently in the mood to admit it.

But for all that, his eyes are the same: a deep brown that veers close to black even in the bright light. Filled with too many things when he looks at me.

I shake my head. "It doesn't matter." I can't stay here, but I've seen enough today to understand that I'm out of my element in a way that's almost laughable.

So, first order of business—gather information and see if

there are allies to exploit. Judging by how things went earlier, Azazel is something of a king here. That complicates things, because I can't go over his head to someone more powerful. Still, there are other ways. There are *always* other ways.

I drop the dress on the ground and pull out another dress, one shorter and easier to move in. Just like the first—and all the others I tried on—it fits me perfectly.

It's enough to make me wonder how long Azazel has been planning this: to trick me, to take me away from everything I've ever known. He may have seemed tormented when we spoke just now, but I don't care about his feelings currently. I could shove him out a window with how furious I am.

I yank on a pair of shoes—another perfect fit—and march to the door. He *said* I have free rein of the castle, but we'll see. I try the door and am actually surprised when the handle twists easily in my hand.

The hallway looks different from the last time I stepped out of my room, when I joined the other women also being herded to the auction. I frown and peer around. There are no doors lining the walls here, and the hall turns in a sharp right angle instead of ending in a door. "What the fuck?"

It's possible I am misremembering things in the chaos or I somehow ended up in a different room than the one I started in . . . but I don't think so. I press my fingers to the wall. It's solid, not some magical illusion.

Funny that my mind hardly stumbles over the idea of magic and monsters, but what am I supposed to do? From the moment I woke up, evidence of both has been shoved in my face. Either I'm in a coma and dreaming all this . . . or monsters are real and so are magical bargains and the whole lot.

I pick a direction at random and start walking. The stone underfoot is polished to a gleam but not slippery in the least. The walls are equally polished and bare except for sconces that must be magic because their flames give off no heat or scent. Neat trick.

I'm not really thinking about my path, just taking the only route available to me—left, left, right, left again, right, right, right—until my legs start to ache. Only then do I frown and look around. I haven't seen a single door or staircase. "What kind of building plan is this?"

It doesn't make any sense. No builder would make a hallway like this. I'm hardly an expert at architecture and the like, but hallways exist for a purpose—to transition from one space to another. Often from one place to *several* others. To have one so long and strange without a single exit defies belief.

Magic, again. It has to be.

While glaring at the hallway, I press my fingers to the wall. Surely there's some illusion in place hiding alternate paths from me. I just have to figure out the trick. "I want to find the kitchen, damn it." With my hand dragging lightly along the wall, I set off walking again.

Except when I turn the next corner, I find a familiar door with a covered tray in front of it. Somehow, despite all logic, I'm back at my room again.

CHAPTER 5

AZAZEL

"The castle is fucking with her. It has been for days."

I press my fingers to my eyes and spend a fruitless moment wishing circumstances were anything but what they are. "The castle fucks with everyone." It's not, strictly speaking, the truth. I'm not in the mood for the truth. Just like I'm not in the mood to have what promises to be an uncomfortable conversation. "Leave it alone, Ramanu."

Ramanu saunters over and perches a hip on my desk. "When were you going to tell me that you signed a *lifetime* contract with her?"

I should feel comfort that Eve is speaking to someone at all, even if that someone isn't me. Instead, jealousy sinks bloody thorns into me. I want Eve to talk to me the way she used to. I'm truly a fool, because I want the connection we shared to be real. It's obviously not on her end; it never was. Even if she'd held some small fondness for me, I annihilated the chance of that growing into more when I brought her here. "I'm not in the mood to entertain this conversation."

"Azazel." Ramanu's tone is uncharacteristically serious. "If there's danger that stretches beyond the human realm, I should be apprised of it."

I'm not fucking *sure* it extends past the human realm. Every step I've made has ensured that my enemies will find no traction in the other territories here. But mine? There's plenty of bargainers who would rather go back to the way things were when Caesarea ruled. When we took what we wanted and damned all the rest. When we didn't *share* power. "Brosh has graduated from posturing to actual threats. I have it on good authority that he was in New York, and there's only one reason for him to be there."

They sigh. "You should have told me. I'm entertaining, and a delightful asshole, but I'm *good* at my job."

It's true. They're the one who will be checking in on the other humans in the various territories over the next seven years. They're the only one I trust to hold the other leaders to the same standards I would. "Do you have everything lined up for the Shadow Market?" As much help as it is to have Ramanu here, I can't keep them from this particular trip.

"Of course. She'll summon me before the event, without a doubt. She's so desperate, I can taste it across the realms."

A witch will be a valued addition to the territory, which is to say nothing of the fact that Ramanu clearly has a soft spot for her. "Just be careful."

They grin. "Darling, I'm never careful."

I stand slowly and stretch. I've been at my desk for most of the day, and my back feels like it's compressed into an unfortunate curve. "Try to act against type for once." Something in my spine pops. "And good luck with your murderous witch."

Their grin widens. "I don't need luck. She's all but mine." They start to turn away. "It's been days, Azazel. You should stop avoiding your human. She's furious and determined enough to try to descend the side of the tower if left to her own devices for too long."

"I already asked the castle to lead her to dinner tonight. I'll take care of it."

Ramanu is still for several long seconds. Finally, they shrug. "It's your funeral. I'll let the kitchen staff know to expect a mess."

"You are such a pain in the ass."

"Want to fire me?" They laugh. "Oh wait, I'm the best at this job, and part of said job is telling you things you don't want to— but need to—hear."

I wave that away. "Go."

"Consider me gone." They pause. "I know you're trying to go easy on her, Azazel, but I think she may surprise you if you're just honest with her."

I don't answer. What is there to say? No amount of honesty will detract from the lies that brought us to this place. *My* lies. "I'll talk to her."

Ramanu snorts. "Good luck."

I wait a bare five minutes after they leave to make my way to my bedroom. The castle isn't particularly pleased with me either; it takes me three times as long to reach my destination. I pause outside my door. "I'm working on it. I'm sorry." There's no response, but why would there be?

Within an hour, I'm in the formal dining room, staring down at two places set. There's no reason for my stomach to be tying itself in knots. I've dealt with so many stressful meetings with greater potential consequences and never once let something as mundane as nerves affect me.

But the personal stakes have never felt higher.

I hear Eve's footsteps before I see her, angry heels clicking on the stone floor. Seconds later, she walks through the doorway looking like a fucking dream. She's wearing a red dress that ties around her neck; the V shows off her generous breasts, making it seem like one wrong move will free them entirely. It's also short—shorter than anything I've seen her wear, barely covering the lower curve of her ass and also showcasing her thick thighs and gently curved calves. Tall heels complete the image.

Her blond hair is loose around her shoulders, styled in waves I want to sink my claws into. Her lips are the same brilliant red as her dress, and her eyes are smokey . . . and furious.

She stops just inside the door and takes me in with a long sweep of her gaze. She crosses to the table and grabs the bottle of wine sitting there. "I was wondering about something. You speak English here. That seems odd."

Guilt pricks me, but there's no point in avoiding this. It will just be worse in the end. "We don't." When she pauses, I force myself to continue. "While you were unconscious, I put a translation spell on you."

"*Put* a translation spell on me."

I swallow hard. "I tattooed it. It's on the back of your neck."

Her eyes flash. "I see." She pours the wine into her glass, filling it nearly to the brim. "I want to go home."

"That's not possible."

She drains half the glass in a single gulp and refills it. "Then I want to know why. You owe me the truth, don't you think? You lied and manipulated and had me sign a contract under false pretenses that took me away from my life, my friends, my fucking *realm*, apparently. The very least you can do is tell me why."

She's right. I know she's right. But telling her the truth is going to make things worse. There's no other option. I watch her lift the wineglass to her ruby lips. "Slow down."

"I don't think I will."

Guilt pricks me, sharp and condemning. "You have a one-drink rule."

"That was for clients, a group that you no longer belong to. I think you'll find that, if I can't control anything else in my life right now, I *can* control this." She holds my gaze as she takes another long drink. It's from one of the cases we imported from the human realm rather than the faerie wine we brew here in this realm, so at least she's not falling-down drunk after a single glass. Even so, I have no idea how often Eve drank or what her tolerance is. So much in so little time is worrisome.

"Eve."

"Answer the fucking question!"

I lower the hand I was lifting to grab the wine bottle. "You're in danger."

"Danger." She sneers. "Do better. More details. I know how well you like to talk, Azazel. So *talk*."

"Time moves differently in this realm than it does in yours." I hold up my hand again, this time to forestall more angry words. "I'm answering your question. This context is necessary."

She pulls out her chair and sinks into it, crossing one leg over the other. "Get to the point."

"The point is that I've been leader of this territory for five years. My predecessor had a markedly different way of doing things; her priority was to gain humans, which resulted in gaining power for our territory. It didn't matter how bargains were made, only that they were. I put a stop to that when I took over."

She lifts an eyebrow. "Until me."

Guilt stabs deeper, but I muscle past it. "There are those among my people who aren't happy with the changes. They think I weakened us, that I'm making the other territories strong at the expense of our own. Caesarea is gone, but many of her supporters remain." I take a breath. "The primary threat is Brosh. He's always been vocal in his criticism of me, but he's decided to take action."

She blinks. "What does that have to do with me?" Before I have a chance to respond, she makes the leap. "It's because you've been one of my clients. A regular. This Brosh decided to get to you through me."

It feels like I'm being suffocated. Fuck, I didn't want to tell her like this. I didn't want to tell her at all. "Yes. The moment I learned he was in New York, I went to you. To protect you."

"How does the time difference work with—" She shakes her head. "You know what, I don't care."

"You're safe here, Eve. No one gets into this castle without my permission."

"I wouldn't need to be safe if you hadn't been playing human for *years* with me." She glares. "Tell him I mean nothing to you. Tell him it was just business and getting your rocks off. Tell him it's all bullshit."

I can't. "It would be a lie."

"It would be a lie," she echoes. "Don't tell me you fell for your own bullshit. Hooker with a heart of gold, right? That's the fairy tale. That it's not a job for me, that I really care about you, that I never once faked it. But you were a damned client and *that is my job.*"

Each word lashes me. "It doesn't matter if I'm a job to you, Eve. He knows me well enough to know that I care about you, so he'll hurt you to punish me. No matter what you feel for me —or don't—you don't deserve to be hurt."

She holds my gaze. "Style yourself my savior in your head, but did you stop to wonder if lying to me, taking me away from everything I've ever known . . . might hurt me too?"

I knew it would. I chose to do it anyway. "Better you be hurt and alive than hurt and dead."

She shakes her head and plants her hands on the table, then propels herself to her feet. "You're lying."

Now it's my turn to blink. "Excuse me?"

"It may be true that Brosh wants me dead, but it's not the full truth, is it?" She drains her wine and sets the glass down on the table. "If you were such a good leader, such a selfless person, then you would have given me a short contract to keep me safe until you had dealt with the situation. Then you would have sent me home." She stands and moves around the table to lean against it, bare inches from me. "But you didn't do that, did you?"

I don't know where to look. Her breasts are so close to my face. The angle of her body makes her dress ride up to truly indecent heights. Her expression is downright dangerous. I push my chair back a little, just to give myself space to think. "Brosh isn't the only threat, just the most present one. Now that my feelings for you are out in the open, the threats won't stop coming."

"Liar." She kicks my legs wide; I'm shocked enough to let her. Eve steps between my thighs and plants her hands on my chest. "You saw an opportunity and you took it." She slides her hands down my stomach and hooks the bottom of my shirt, then reverses direction and lifts it. "You wanted me forever, didn't you?"

Of course I did. How could I not? I jerk my gaze to her furious eyes. "I may have lied to you before, but I won't in the future. Not again. I promise."

"Whatever you say." She leans forward but has to practically crawl into my lap to reach the sensitive spot beneath my ear. "Well, I'm here. Take me."

I freeze. "Stop that."

But she doesn't stop. She straddles my hips, revealing a tiny slice of red fabric covering her pussy. It's so thin, I can see her slit through it. My cock jumps. I can't help it. I grab her hips. "Eve."

"Tell me your safe word, Azazel." The snap in her voice makes my cock even harder. My sexual tastes are varied, but Eve fits them all. She always has. She grabs my chin and forces me to meet her furious dark eyes. "Now."

"Apple," I grit out.

"Do you want to use it, Daddy?" She doesn't move her body, but her nails prick my skin.

I know what the right answer is. Speak the word and put a stop to her doing this for all the wrong reasons. The problem is that I can't find the breath to speak at all. I've seen her unwound and messy and orgasming, but this feels like the first time I've seen all *Eve*, not the bits she allows through the shield of Ginger.

Eve narrows her eyes and drags her gaze over my features. "If you won't say it, then answer a question, Daddy: Do you want me to stop?"

It turns out I *do* have the breath for words. "Why call me that?" I never would have said it's a particular kink of mine, but on Eve's lips?

"You have me grounded here. I can't leave. You control every element of my life now. Who does that if not a Daddy?" She drags her thumb over my bottom lip. "It makes me want to put you in your place the only way I can. And you like it. I can feel that you do."

I do like it. Entirely too much. I swallow hard. "You'll hate me." Each word fights against her grip on my chin.

"I already hate you, Daddy." She finally moves, rolling her hips to grind herself over my hard cock. The weight of her, the friction against *me*, not through the shield of a glamor, is nearly enough to have me coming right here and now. But as soon as she starts, she stops. "So be it." She starts to rise.

I tighten my grip on her hips and slam her back down onto me. "I don't want you to stop. Even if you hate me."

CHAPTER 6

EVE

I know this is a mistake, but I don't care. I've spent days wandering the halls of this cursed castle, my frustration and fury growing with each turn that leads me nowhere but to another endless hall until I'm finally deposited back at my bedroom.

If I had better control, I would come up with some kind of brilliant plan to seduce my way to freedom. I know what Azazel likes—at least what he's shown me so far. But right now, looking up at his ruggedly handsome face, crimson skin blushing darker with lust, eyes gone obsidian when I called him *Daddy* . . .

It's hard to think of anything at all.

Instead of fighting it, I allow myself to fall. I've done nothing but *think* for days. I'm exhausted, frustrated, and heartsore. I thought my days of using sex as a way to purge messy emotions were over, that those more dangerous impulses were carefully caged, but apparently some scars run too deep. When faced with a situation I have no hope of controlling, I slide right back into being that girl who held her aching heart outside her chest, who took a razor blade to it before anyone else had a chance to, just to know that no one else could hurt her worse than she hurt herself.

"Eve."

"No." I dig my nails into Azazel's square jaw. He's so fucking *big* in this form. He was already significantly taller than me, but now he has *feet* over my five foot five inches and his body is built like the strongmen who toss around boulders and trees for prestige. I swallow hard. "I don't want to hear you say a single thing unless it's your safe word." A word we negotiated before my first night with him. It's a required step for all my clients, even if we're not engaging in kink. A little fail-safe for my peace of mind—and theirs.

I don't really care if Azazel has peace of mind right now, but no matter how close my fury flirts with hatred, there are lines that should never be crossed. I won't respect a single word out of his mouth . . . except that one.

His hands bracket my hips, the strength there enough to make my skin prickle, but he doesn't attempt to control or maneuver me as I grind down on his cock. His truly, world-endingly huge cock. Historically, I've scoffed at the idea that anyone would be too large to fit, but I truly don't know how he will without ripping me in half.

Good thing I'm in the mood for pain.

I cling to his shoulders, using my thighs to maintain my place, and nip his earlobe. It shouldn't be so sexy, but there are a lot of things about this that shouldn't be so sexy. I release his jaw and grip his horn, earning a muffled curse. "You want to play Daddy and take care of me, Azazel?" I lick the shell of a delicately pointed ear. "Then *take care of me*."

He doesn't hesitate. One moment, I'm doing my best to straddle his stomach. The next, he bands his forearm under my ass and uses his free hand to sweep both place settings from the table. The bottle crashes to the stone, sending up the strong scent of wine. A loss, but I'm too busy being laid out on the table as if *I'm* the feast to worry about it. The glass and a half that I drank makes my body fizzle, but I'm nowhere near drunk. That would be too easy.

Azazel plants a hand next to my hip, towering over me for all that he's bent nearly in half. I never thought I'd be one to have a size kink—or a hate-sex kink—but I can't deny the way my pussy pulses in response.

My dress is tangled around my waist, exposing my thong. He makes a sound deliriously close to a true growl and rips it off. It's such a smooth move that my hips don't even jerk. With one last look at my face, he goes to his knees.

On his knees and with me sitting on the table, we're nearly the same height. He yanks down my dress and palms my breasts, but there's no savoring the movement the way there has been historically. The fury that drives me . . . Well, I can't tell if it's present in him or not, only that he's *intense* in way that leaves no room for softness.

Good. I want none.

He plants one giant hand on my chest and pushes me down onto my back. Then he dips down and . . . Holy shit, he hooks my thighs over his horns, spreading them wide and exposing me fully.

I open my mouth to command him to do . . . something. Something that will put me back in control. Something that will make me feel less vulnerable.

I never get that chance. He covers my pussy with his mouth and kisses me with a frenzy that makes my eyes roll back in my head. I writhe on instinct, not sure if I'm trying to get away from the slick slide of his long tongue or arch closer. Azazel doesn't allow me to decide. He palms my ass, lifting my hips even as his horns press my thighs wider.

He thrusts his tongue into my pussy; it's nearly as thick and long as a cock but able to curl against my G-spot. I cry out, my words garbled with need. "MorePleaseDon'tstop!" I don't know how he understands me, but he does.

He doesn't stop. He keeps working me with his tongue as pressure builds, pulling my body tighter and tighter. I reach out wildly and my hands find his horns, then hold on with everything they have. And then I'm coming, the orgasm hitting me with the strength of a rogue wave, unexpected and violent.

Azazel eases his tongue out of me but doesn't move away. He kisses my pussy as if he can't get enough the taste, as if he never wants to stop. He nuzzles one thigh and then the other, nipping me lightly in the way I like sometimes, before moving back to roll the flat of his tongue against my clit.

This was a mistake.

I can't find the breath to say so, to tell him to stop. That's why I grip his horns tighter, why I arch closer. Not because I want to. Not because I know what comes next, how he can go for hours, alternating his attention so that I'm never quite overstimulated to the point of commanding him to stop instead of begging for more.

My second orgasm seems to build on the first. And then the third adds even more. And on and on, until I'm wrung out and limp, my hands falling to the table as I blink up at the stone ceiling.

"This was a mistake," I rasp.

He moves back instantly. Azazel carefully disentangles my legs from his horns and stands. He cups my face, his gentleness unwanted, and yet . . . I close my eyes and lean against his palm. Just a little.

The moment I realize what I've done, I try to retreat. Azazel is already moving, scooping me into his arms. I've never felt so small in my life, and if there's a part of me that wants to nuzzle up to him, it's only the post-orgasm haze confusing my senses. "Put me down."

He ignores me, walking out of the room and through the

halls with what feels like dizzying speed. Or maybe it just feels that way, since spare moments later he's shouldering open the familiar door to my bedroom.

I expect—dread, hope for—him to enter the room, lay me on the bed, and continue what we started. Instead, he sets me on my feet and holds my shoulders until he's sure I'm steady. I wish I were as sure. My body feels like it belongs to someone else, limbs loose and heart pounding. I look up at him, and if there's any consolation to how shaken I am, it's that Azazel appears equally so. His chest rises and falls with harsh breathing, and his cock is a long line against his pants.

I swallow. "You—"

He cups my cheek again, something in his eyes that I can't quite define. "Hate me if you must, Eve. Punish me all you like. I can take it." He kisses me, the lightest brush of his lips against mine, and then takes one large step away and then another. "Have dinner with me tomorrow."

I can't corral my racing thoughts enough to *think*. "Stay." I blink up at him as if he summoned the word against my will. Surely I didn't just expose myself in this horribly vulnerable way.

He doesn't close the distance, doesn't stop his retreat. "Not tonight, Eve. Not like this." Then he goes, shutting the door softly behind him.

Leaving me alone.

I hate how my heart drops in my chest. I hate how it feels like he's rejecting me when I'm the one who set the tone for the night. I especially hate how it feels like I set out to punish him but only ended up punishing myself.

Seconds tick by, my body cooling even though my heart rate isn't returning to anywhere close to normal. He could have fucked me until dawn, and I wouldn't have done anything but beg him for more.

And through it all, he didn't disobey me once. He didn't

speak. He didn't push. He simply gave, paying penance with his mouth despite our mutual desire for more.

It doesn't make sense for his restraint to make me even angrier. It's not fair—I can recognize that—but I'm not in the mood to be fair. Not anytime in this century.

I march into the bathroom and wrench on the shower. Because of course they have indoor plumbing in the fucking demon realm, and I loathe that I'm grateful for it. I yank off my rumpled dress and step beneath the blistering spray. I press my hands to the tiled wall and duck my head, letting the water cascade over me, blocking out the rest of the world. All of it does little to reset my mind and emotions.

This accomplished nothing. Pleasure usually unwinds me, but I'm more tense than when I marched to dinner, ready to fight. I sigh and shut off the water. I don't know what I'm more pissed about. That Azazel just made me come until my body went limp . . . or that he walked away. It shouldn't matter. I hate him for what he's done; wanting him to choose me is a fool's game. Unfortunately, that lost little girl inside me, the one who was always passed over, time and time again, is a ghost I can never quite vanquish. It hurts to be left. Far more than it should.

An enticing scent reaches me as I towel off. My heart picks up. "Azazel?" There's no answer. Why would there be? He *left*, and I know it's not fair to blame him for it, but again, I'm not in the mood to be fair right now.

Back in my bedroom, I find a covered tray sitting on the desk. A peek shows a steaming-hot dinner. No wine, which makes my lips quirk despite myself. "You are such an over-bearing asshole." My smile fades away. I don't know what to do. I don't see a way out of this.

Worst of all, lust still coats my skin, demanding more, more, more.

CHAPTER 7

EVE

I'm ashamed to say I hide for days after that disastrous dinner. Azazel comes to my door several times and knocks as politely as if he were a suitor instead of my captor. And he just as politely leaves when he receives no answer.

There's no reason for that to upset me further. I should be grateful for the reprieve. Should be pleased that no matter what else is true, he doesn't intend to take advantage of the power dynamic.

No, that's all on me. I'm the one who climbed in his lap and demanded something I knew would hurt us both. And the bastard gave it to me without hesitation—only to leave me wanting more.

By the third day, I'm sick of my own company, my relentlessly spinning thoughts. I pull on a pair of pants, a long shirt that could probably be termed a tunic, and some boots I found tucked in the bottom of the wardrobe.

"I don't care how long it takes. I'm getting out of this magic trap of a hallway." I glare at the room around me. "You have to let me out at some point!"

But when I throw open my door, it's to find Ramanu waiting for me. They're wearing a boxy cropped top that leaves their stomach bare, a garment that may be pants or may be a skirt, and boots. They grin. "Perfect timing."

I narrow my eyes. "Perfect timing for what?"

"Azazel is tied up in meetings today, and I figured you could use a change of scenery." They offer me their arm. "Let's go shopping."

"Shopping . . ."

They don't wait for me to move; they loop their arm through mine and turn us down the hall. "Yes, Eve. Everyone loves shopping. It's an excellent way to pass the time, and there's something to be said for seeing the very people Azazel has fought so hard to make a better life for."

I shoot them a glare. "So we get to the crux of the matter. You're here to campaign for your boss."

"I campaign for no one, darling. It sounds like a staggering amount of effort with little fun involved." We turn a corner, and I could sob in relief at the sight of wide stone stairs leading downward. Ramanu laughs a little. "The castle is wary of strangers. It helps if you're polite in the first place, rather than cursing at it."

"You speak as if it's a person."

"Not quite." They shrug. "But magic is a strange thing and it never hurts to be courteous when dealing with borderline sentient objects and places."

"I wouldn't know," I murmur. Up until the moment I woke up here, I assumed magic was fiction. Yes, this world—or my world—is complicated and strange, but hundreds of years ago, they were calling things like antibiotics witchcraft and no one washed their hands. If there's magic, then it's just science that we don't have the technology or knowledge to explain yet.

It's hard to keep that belief when faced with a castle that seems to shift itself at will.

I don't think science can explain *that*.

We walk down the stairs and then down another set and another. I haven't worked out in a week, and I'd love to believe that my endurance wouldn't flatline as a result, but my thighs are shaking by the time Ramanu stops and tilts their head to the side. "Castle, please. You're being difficult for no reason. I'm not absconding with her. We're going on a nice little walk to let the sun touch her face, and then I'll return her, safe and sound." They snort. "You've being overprotective."

"Overprotective of whom?" Surely not Azazel. He's more than capable of taking care of himself.

"Ah, here we are." Ramanu turns me to face the staircase . . . except it's gone. Instead, there's a narrow hallway that ends in double doors.

I shudder. "I am never going to get used to that."

"You'd be surprised."

I don't have a chance to come up with a response to that, because we walk out the doors and into another world. One strange and yet familiar at the same time. I've traveled widely, and if every city I've visited has a different feel, they all share certain things in common—the main of which is a large variety of people moving about their day with a rhythm that feels almost coordinated.

These people aren't human. They have skin tones that range from a rosy pink to a deep crimson that edges into black. Their horns are different shapes and sizes. Some of them have wings tucked politely against their backs, some have dual sets of horns like Ramanu, and some even have scales like the dragon-man who attended the auction. They're tall and short, fat and skinny and brawny, and everything in between. Some of them are clothed similarly to me. Some are wearing dresses. Others are wearing pants or kilts and little else.

And there are humans mixed in among them.

I try not to stare as Ramanu leads me down a cobblestone

street that seems designated for foot traffic only. I see a willowy Black human with short curls and warm dark-brown skin. There's a short white human with pale pink skin, a long blond hair, and the kind of curves that make my mouth water. And more. So many more.

And the children. I don't know why it shocks me to see them walking side by side with people who may be parents or guardians. Or the small group in an open courtyard we walk past, darting about and laughing wildly as they play some game I don't recognize with two balls. The sound rolls through me, easing something tight in my stomach. These children are happy. They're *safe*. Safe enough to be comfortable being loud and rambunctious.

I'm not naive. I understand all too well that this is a small sliver of the population. Surely abuse and neglect exist here just like they do in my world . . . but it's hard not to slow, wanting to linger in this moment of peace.

"I would like an explanation," I say softly. "Not for what Azazel did—for how this works. Because it sure seems like your people take advantage of mine."

Ramanu snorts. "There was a time when that might have been true, but Azazel put a stop to it. We only offer bargains to those who want them, and they're fair enough deals when all is said and done. Anything within our power to grant in exchange for seven years in this realm with safeguards in place to ensure no one is forced to do anything."

"The power dynamics—"

They stop short, stopping me alongside them. "In the human world, you would be right. There are power dynamics at play, and they can be abused readily. Not here. The contract is sacred, Eve. I don't mean that as a metaphor. Both parties sign it, and it's *binding*. To violate it is to nullify it."

Nullify.

I tuck that knowledge away to examine later. If I can force

Azazel into breaking the contract, that will nullify the terms and force him to take me home . . . hopefully. Ramanu mentioned something about this when we spoke earlier, but I wasn't willing to listen then. I am now.

"Seven years is a long time," I finally say.

"Yes and no." Ramanu shrugs. "Time moves differently from realm to realm. It's not an exact science, more like two rivers running next to each other at different speeds. You can jump from one to the other, and it feels like you haven't moved at all. We bargainers have a little control over where we land, which means we can return our humans to a place and time not too distant from where they left. The magic in this realm also slows aging, so you're not actually losing time at all. It's more as if you've gained the years—and what you've gained, you've spent here. Then you return home, none the worse for wear and with whatever you wanted enough to bargain for in the first place. Win-win."

I suspect they're intentionally simplifying things and leaving a few key details out. Like the fact that someone would have to be in a desperate situation to think that making a deal with a demon is a legitimate strategy.

Ramanu seems to know everyone, smiling and calling folks by name as I meander the aisles. This, at least, is familiar. I love shopping. Gaining new clothes or necessities was always a burden as a foster kid. I was with a handful of families growing up, and while none of them were the stuff of horror stories, there was never enough to go around. Once I started making the kind of money I do now, I went a little wild with the spending. At least until Pope found out I was getting myself into trouble and sat me down with a financial advisor. The impulse to spend and spend and spend, to surround myself with expensive and beautiful things, never quite went away, but I have better control now.

And a wicked investment portfolio.

Not that any of *that* matters here.

"Would you like it?"

I jolt and glance at Ramanu. They nod to the bracelet I've been fondling. I shake my head and set it back down. "I don't have money."

"Eve."

The censor in their tone irritates me. I glare. "I realize that you offered to take me shopping, and if you were one of my clients, I'd allow you to pay through the nose for whatever I want, but you're not."

They sigh. "Neither is Azazel, currently, but we're shopping with *his* funds." Ramanu nudges me with their shoulder. "Are you sure you don't want to stick it to him, just a little?"

My pride wants to ignore the offer, but that would only deny me the pretty things in this place—and the chance to make Azazel hurt, even a little. Though I suspect I'd have to buy out every shop in the city for him to feel the pinch. I pick up the bracelet again. It's an intricate creation with a rainbow of gemstones. Bright and shiny and loud. I love it. "Fine. I suppose I could find a few things."

"That's the spirit."

We walk for hours, visiting shops and chatting easily. I expect to have to carry bags, but Ramanu arranges for my purchases to be delivered directly to the castle. It frees me up to watch the city's citizens. Again and again, I'm struck by how familiar this all is despite how strange the people appear to me. But they're just people, aren't they? Citizens of this city going about their business by shopping, eating, socializing, working.

Despite myself, I can't help seeing why Azazel would want to protect this. If Ramanu isn't overstating the direness of the situation before he took over, this *wasn't* how people acted before. They've benefited from Azazel's rule.

We're nibbling on some kind of street food that's a bit like a kebob with vegetables I don't recognize when Ramanu straightens. "Damn. Duty calls."

I know better than to ask if I can keep wandering. I'm not ready to go back to my richly appointed cell yet, but what does that matter? I sigh and take the last bite of my food, then follow Ramanu to a garbage bin to toss the stick into. "Can we do this again sometime?"

They turn their face to me. Not for the first time, I'm struck by the suspicion that they see me just fine despite not having eyes in the traditional manner. "You know, you could ask Azazel to take you. It would get him out of the castle, which would do him some good."

"I am not interested in what would be good for Azazel," I say primly.

"He's not a bad man." Ramanu guides us through the thickening foot traffic with ease. "Not in the way you think. He'd kill, burn, and maim to protect his people and his humans, but he doesn't abuse his power. He's sharing power for the good of the realm. For all its peoples—not just the bargainers. That's got some folks' backs up, but it won't stop his pursuit of the greater good."

"Folks like Brosh?"

Ramanu almost misses a step. They've been so graceful to date, it's like a record scratch. "I would prefer you don't say that name outside the castle."

"Is he like some kind of boogeyman? Speak his name three times and he appears?"

"No. Nothing so dramatic. But he has an irritating number of supporters in the city and beyond. There's no reason to draw attention to ourselves." Their tone is breezy, but contains a new tension that makes me think there's more going on than what they're saying.

The castle looms large in front of us. It truly is like something out of a fairy tale. I don't know what kind of rock it's made of, but the rock almost a cross between granite and opal, strong and gorgeous, gleaming with a dazzling rainbow of colors in the late-afternoon sun. "It's beautiful."

"It's home," Ramanu says simply.

We're almost within the shadow of the castle when they stop so abruptly, my shoulder wrenches from our still-interlocked arms. "Ow."

"Get behind me." They don't wait for me to comply. With a smooth move, they free themself and shove me behind them. Ramanu is taller than me by about half a foot. And they're built significantly leaner than Azazel, so I have no problem seeing around their shoulder to where two massive bargainers stand blocking our way.

The largest of them has wings, and I catch myself wondering if this was the same person I saw flying on my first day here. Surely not. That would be too large of a coincidence. They're even larger than Azazel—apparently the metric I judge everyone by these days—and wear only a kilt around their thick waist.

The other is closer to Ramanu's size, lean like a blade, with curving ram's horns that bracket their long straight dark hair. They grin, revealing too-sharp teeth. "Hand her over or this gets messy."

Ramanu laughs, loud and pretty. "I think not."

"We have no issue with you, Ramanu," the larger one says. "Stand aside."

There's a faint *shtck* sound like a blade being drawn. My heart leaps into my throat when I realize what it is. Ramanu's claws. They were petite and black, but now they're curved and look vicious enough to disembowel someone.

Any hope I had of this being all posturing and bullshit disappears. Ramanu may be dramatic, but they've shown no signs of being unnecessarily violent. They wouldn't issue this unspoken threat if they didn't mean it.

As if sensing my growing fear, they turn their head enough to speak to me over their shoulder. "Don't run. They'll have a third waiting to snatch you if you do. Stay close."

I don't know if they mean to reassure me, but I am very much *not* reassured. "You can't take three of them on," I hiss. "We have to run."

"I have no intention of taking three of them on," they murmur. "I'm stalling."

"Stall—" The word dies in my throat as the double doors to the castle slam open with a violence that seems to shake the entire square we stand in. People hadn't seemed to register the growing possibility of a fight before, but they scatter now, rushing away from us or taking refuge in the stores on either side. In seconds, the square is empty but for the two—three— attackers, Ramanu, and I.

A huge form fills the doorway, and I let out a sound of pure relief at the familiar sight of wide shoulders and horns as he steps into the fading light.

Azazel is here.

CHAPTER 8

AZAZEL

I take in the scene with a single sweep. Three strangers. Ramanu doing their best to shield Eve. It won't work. There are too many, and Ramanu isn't trained as a bodyguard. I catch their eye and nod. The moment I got their signal—a little magical panic button that all my people carry when out in the world—I rushed here. I'm only glad I'm not too late.

Time to even the odds.

I barrel into the pair closest to me. The bigger one with wings dodges my swipe, but I catch the other in the throat and close my fingers around their neck. It would take nothing at all to change my grip, to rip out their fucking throat for daring to threaten what's mine. Only the knowledge that we need whatever information they have on Brosh stays my hand.

That . . . and the desire for Eve not to view me as more of a monster than she already does.

Instead, I toss them through the doors and into the castle. "Dungeon!"

The doors slams shut for a brief moment. When they open

again, only the empty hallway remains. Good. Now for the other two.

The one behind Ramanu and Eve rushes them, pulling a blade from their robes. Fear lodges itself in my chest. "Knife!" I roar.

"I see," Ramanu snaps. They grab Eve's arm and send her barreling behind them as they move to meet the attacker. I don't have cause to see them fight often, but gods, they're vicious and brutal. They break the bargainer's wrist, snatch the knife, and plunge it into their enemy's stomach. Then they twist it for good measure.

Eve's shriek brings me back around. The winged bargainer has their arms around her and is tensing to launch into the air.

"No!"

I lunge just as they take off, getting a hand around their calf, but the panicked batting of their wings makes them lurch higher, sending my grip sliding down to their ankle.

I can take them out of the sky, but not without endangering Eve. "Ramanu!" I hold out my free hand, bracing as well as I can. "Get Eve!"

My second-in-command sprints to us and steps into my offered palm without missing a beat, and I use all my strength to toss them up. Their momentum works well, as does our enemy's desperation. Ramanu snatches Eve right out of their arms as they fly over the bargainer's head. The second they're clear, I grab the unknown bargainer's leg with both hands and slam them down on the ground hard enough to shatter the cobblestones beneath my feet. The crunch of their bones is so loud that I know they won't be getting up again.

Ramanu lands lightly behind me, Eve safely in their arms. "That was eventful."

I survey the two dead bodies. "You didn't have to twist the knife."

"You already have one captive. No need to waste resources

with more." They set Eve carefully on her feet. "Besides, you needed my assistance."

But I'm not listening any longer. I go to Eve, staring at the bloodshed with wide eyes, her face gone too pale. She's safe now, but she won't believe it. Not yet. I sweep her into my arms. "Get this cleaned up," I call over my shoulder.

"Of course."

My tension doesn't leave as I step through the doorway and back into the relative safety of the castle. Eve is shaking, her eyes too wide and her hand convulsively gripping my shirt. "You're safe," I say softly. "Eve, you're safe."

"You said you would stop lying."

The castle understands my urgency, because there's only a single staircase and a short hallway before I'm pushing through the door into Eve's suite. "I'm not lying. You're safe now. I won't let anyone hurt you." I walk past the bed and into the bathroom. I don't think she's noticed the blood on her shirt, and I want to get it off before she does. She's not quite panicking, but there's no reason to traumatize her further. "I'm sorry you had to experience that. I misjudged their boldness, or I wouldn't have let you and Ramanu out of here without an escort."

"Azazel." She presses her hand to my chest, her brown eyes serious. The earlier shakiness seems to be easing, tucking itself away where she can deal with it privately. I wish she trusted me enough to let me share that burden with her, but I've done little to deserve her trust at this point. She drops her hand. "I am so angry with you that I can barely put it into words. But there's no way you could have known we'd be in danger in what amounts to your front yard. Stop flogging yourself."

"You could flog me instead." Damn it, I didn't mean to say that. I don't mean to do a lot of things around Eve.

Her eyes flash. "Absolutely not. There are lines, and I don't trust myself not to cross them with how I'm feeling these days."

We did very little kink on the nights I contracted with her. I didn't have the patience for it, couldn't think past the frenzy she inspires in me. My desire is still there, barely tempered beneath the surface. I'm still not certain how I managed to keep from fucking her the other night on the dining room table. My need was—is—a live thing inside me, chanting a single word over and over again. *Eve.* No one else will do.

In the past, I've laughed at the dragons for being so stringent with their rituals of courtship and marriage. I think I understand it better now. I want Eve as *mine.* My ring on her finger if that human ritual is what she needs. Her standing before my people as co-ruler . . .

But that's a fool's dream.

She may not have faked her orgasms with me, but as she's so keen to remind me, everything else was a job to her. She doesn't share the emotional attachment I have, and I'm a fool for developing one in the first place.

None of that matters right now. "Let me take care of you." I keep my voice low and even. "Just until you feel steadier on your feet. Please, Eve."

She opens her mouth, obviously intent on denying us both, but finally sighs. "It means nothing."

"I know." I set her down on the stool next to the tub and reach past her to get the water going. There's nothing else to say. I need to question the single enemy left alive. If I can find where Brosh is hiding, can figure out exactly how extensive the network of betrayal is . . .

But that's a problem for later. Right now, there's a woman who will never be mine in truth who has agreed to accept my care.

The tub fills fast. I reach for her shirt, but pause. "May I?"

Something flickers across her face that's *almost* humor. "Azazel, you've seen me naked more times than I care to count. Don't tell me you're getting shy *now.*"

There are dozens of answers to that, none of them good

enough to speak. Instead, I carefully pull her shirt over her head —and freeze at the sight of the bruise already darkening across her ribs. I drift my fingers through the air above the purple-and-green mark from where the bargainer held her as they tried to escape. "I have something that will help this if you'll allow it."

"Considering it hurts enough to make breathing difficult, I wouldn't say no to medical care."

"Don't move." I walk to the cabinet and dig through the drawers until I come up with the balm that was designed . . . Well, best not to think of that right now. No matter its intended use, it's still good for surface-level injuries of all varieties, and while it won't get to the deeper parts of the bruise right away, it will help her pain levels.

I return to where Eve sits and crouch in front of her. It puts her breasts at face level, which would be easier to ignore if the bruise didn't stretch across her ribs just beneath her gloriously full . . . Stop. "Can you lift your arms over your head?"

In response, she does exactly that, then rests her forearms on the top of her head. My gaze catches on her rosy nipples, and I have to inhale carefully. Damn it, this was a terrible idea. I could have just given her the balm and allowed her to put it on herself. Backing out now isn't an option, though. No matter how ill-advised this is.

I dip my fingers into the balm and carefully drag them over the middle of the bruise. She sucks in a surprised breath. "It tingles."

"I know." I do my very damnedest to not think about the other ways that tingle can be used to amplify pleasure, to . . . Fuck. I massage the balm into her skin gently, ensuring I don't put too much pressure on the injury.

It takes an eternity. It takes no time at all.

"There." I sit back on my heels and put the lid back on. "Put another coat on it in the morning, and you should be good as new."

"Thanks."

I need to move, to stand, to put some distance between us—not measure the steady rise and fall of her breasts as she breathes. Staying here a moment longer is both the greatest and worst idea in the world. I want to tug off her pants, to scour her body for any further scrapes or bruises. To . . . kiss her better.

As if she could possibly view my touch as anything other than punishment.

I jerk to my feet. "I think you have it from here. I need to question the . . ." Surviving attacker. Saying that will only remind her of my capacity for violence. I never wanted her to see that. I'm not ashamed of the things I've done to protect this territory, this realm, this *woman*, but I do regret that it only further confirms her negative vision of me.

In keeping her safe, I've lost her forever.

As long as she's still breathing, still fighting, then it's a price worth paying. Even if she hates me. Even if she ends up searching out the company of another.

Eve doesn't call me back as I leave the bathroom. I linger outside that door for a few extra beats in hope that she will. But she doesn't.

I swallow my sigh and leave her room, tugging the door gently shut behind me. I pause there. "Go easy on her. It's not her fault that she's upset about being here. She's entitled to feel the way she does about me. And the rest of us can work to be more welcoming."

The castle gives no response, but I don't truly expect one. I head down the hall and then descend a narrow set of stairs to the dungeon. Ramanu is already there, their mouth drawn into a tight line. "We have a problem."

I follow their motion to see a body laid out on the floor. The cause of death is clear enough from the red-flecked foam at their mouth. Poison. "This seems extreme, even for Brosh."

"I agree." They cross their arms over their chest and shift

from foot to foot. "I don't like leaving you and the others. I can postpone—"

"It will be fine," I say with a confidence I don't quite feel. I know how much the murderous little witch intrigues Ramanu, and they've put their interests on hold time and time again to help me. The witch has been gathering supplies to summon them, so it's only a matter of time before she does. I can't hold them back from that, no matter how inconvenient the timing.

They hesitate but finally nod. "How is Eve?"

"Shaken up and bruised, but otherwise fine." *Fine.* Such a neat little word that means absolutely nothing at all. She's not fine. She may never be again. Because of my choices, my selfishness. If I'd taken care of Brosh when I realized he was a problem . . . If I'd demonstrated enough control to stay away from Eve . . .

It's too late to go back now.

I hate that I'm grateful for that fact. I hate that I don't know if I'd make different decisions even if I had the choice to change things. She may hate me, but she's *here*.

I truly am the monster she thinks.

CHAPTER 9

EVE

I can't sleep.

It's not the bruise, which still radiates a faint ache through my ribs with each breath, that keeps me awake; that's healing faster than I could have imagined. I don't know what magic is in the balm Azazel used, but it works and works well.

It's not that Ramanu unquestionably killed a person right in front of me. For reasons unknown, that doesn't shift my perspective of them at all. Maybe because I don't have a tangled mass of conflicting emotions in my chest when I think of Ramanu. I believe we could be friends, given some time, but I have no desire for more than that with them.

With Azazel?

He killed someone too. Someone who was trying to *take* me. He came running the moment there was trouble, without hesitation. More than that . . . I glare up at my ceiling. This may not be the route I would have chosen, but Azazel is a king. He has so many more lives to worry about than just mine. He could have let his enemy take me. It would have been easy. A preventable death, but it would have closed any weakness for Brosh to exploit.

But he didn't. He saved me. He keeps saving me.

I roll over for the hundredth time, but no matter how comfortable my bed is, I can't escape the thoughts lingering in the back of my mind. I should hate Azazel. I *do* hate him. He's protecting me from danger that his presence created. But the danger is true enough. I don't want to die.

I'm no stranger to stalking or even violence. I wish it were otherwise, but even before I started my work as an escort, there were a string of bad relationships with both men and women. Looking for love in all the wrong places. Or, rather, I was looking for love, and the people I fell for were looking for someone who was less of a partner and more of a possession. After my last girlfriend slit my tires over a harmless text, I swore off dating entirely. Then I met Pope and started my work. I'm too busy to date now, too uninterested in all the bullshit that comes with filtering out potential prospects who would have a problem with what I do.

And if I sometimes develop fondness and desire for my clients? If sometimes I let myself fall into the fantasy that they love me too, that they're choosing me above all others? Well, that's my problem, not theirs.

I'm spiraling, I know I'm spiraling, but I don't know how to stop it. There's no Pope to call to talk through the mess in my head. I know what they would say about my unease with Azazel: Use what you've got. He obviously cares about my well-being, even if he's going about it in a shitty, over the top way. I could use that . . .

God, I'm so tired.

I open my eyes and stare at the city lights dancing over my ceiling with the movement of my sheer curtain in the faint breeze. It's all too much. This situation. The violence I witnessed today. The future. All of it.

I don't make the decision to get out of bed and pull on a short robe. I certainly don't choose to open the door and step into the hallway. The lights are lower than normal, a nod to the late hour.

"I don't know how to do this." I reach out and gingerly press my fingertips to the stone wall. It's cool and pleasing against my skin. "I . . ." I take a deep breath. "I would like to go to Azazel . . . please."

Nothing happens as far as I can tell, but even with Ramanu and Azazel, I never see the castle move. It's one of those strange phenomena where I look away and when I look back, things have changed. With that in mind, I start walking.

This may be all for naught. Or I may change my mind the moment I come up against the reality of how impulsive I'm being. I pick up my pace, as if speed has ever been enough to outrun my thoughts.

Since I've been here, I've tried to leave my room multiple times, and each attempt has been met with frustration. I just walk and walk and walk, and right when I'm at the point of breaking, the damned castle deposits me back in front of my door.

Not so tonight.

The first turn ends in a short hall with a large door. I stop abruptly and narrow my eyes. "Is this a trick?" There's no answer, but why would there be? This castle has no voice. I never found that truly tragic until this moment. I look around and clear my throat. "Uh, thank you. I didn't mean to sound ungrateful."

There's nothing to do but knock on the door and hope for the best. The wood is more textured than I expect at first glance, rough against my knuckles.

Seconds later, the door opens to reveal Azazel. It's late enough that he's traded in his customary tunic and pants for some type of short skirt garment that wraps around his hips and leaves most of his legs bare. His thighs are *huge*. Ruinous, even. I've never wanted to bite thighs the way I suddenly ache to in this moment.

He frowns. "Eve. Is something wrong?"

"Everything's wrong." The words are stark and filled with enough honesty to drown us both. "I can't think, can't sleep. Today was . . ."

"A lot. I know. I'm sorry. I would spare you the memories if I could." He takes a step back, a clear invitation to enter.

Coming to him at all was a terrible idea. I knew it the moment I got out of bed. Sometimes, that's all there is: bad and worse. Staying in my own room and being suffocated by my racing thoughts was worse than whatever this is.

You know what this is.

I guess I do. The moment Azazel shuts the door, I shrug out of my robe. I'm not wearing anything underneath.

His shocked inhale is almost—almost—enough to make me look at him.

"Eve?"

"I can't think anymore." It's suddenly all too much. I close my eyes. "I know this is fucked on so many levels, Azazel. I shouldn't be here."

There's no sound to indicate movement, but when he speaks, his voice comes from in front of me. "Are you doing this to help or to hurt?"

I shrug helplessly. "Both?"

His strained chuckle tugs at something in my chest. I don't want to understand him. I don't want to recognize that he's just as out of his depth right now as I am. I certainly don't want to admit that maybe he's making the best of a shitty situation. "Is it me you want to hurt . . . or yourself?"

"Both," I whisper.

"It's a bad idea." He's closer. I swear I can feel the heat coming off his body now. "Every time I touch you, you resent me more."

If only that were true. If only I hadn't spent every night since that scene in the dining room fingering myself to the memory of him. Not his human version, for all that the sex was outstanding. No, when I slip my hand between my thighs, it's horns, obsidian eyes, and a too-long wicked tongue I'm remembering.

I open my eyes to find him a few measly inches from me. It would be so easy to push this, to take control like I did last time. But . . . I'm tired. Scared. Shaky in a way I don't know how to combat. "Touch me." I suck in a harsh breath. "Please."

As he reaches out to cup my face in his giant hands, I make my peace with the truth—in the morning, it won't be him that I resent. It will be myself. For being weak in my desire. For wanting the person who's responsible for upending my life.

That's a problem for tomorrow.

Right now, Azazel lowers his mouth to mine, kissing me so sweetly, I might weep from the longing that springs to life in my chest. To be a different woman, with different fault lines. To be able to accept this and stop fighting. To do . . . a lot of things.

I break the kiss. "I can't do soft. I—"

He bands an arm under my ass and lifts me until our faces are even. "If at any point you want to stop, say 'stop' and it ends. Do you understand?"

"Yes?"

This time, when he kisses me, it's just short of violent. I moan into his mouth and enter the battle of teeth and tongues. Yes, this—*this* is what I need. He walks us across the room, and it seems to take forever, but I'm not curious enough to stop kissing him. Especially when he finally lays me down on his absurdly soft bed and moves back to kneel between my spread thighs, then undo his loincloth and toss it to the side.

The size difference really is absurd. The tallest person I've ever been with is six-five, and Azazel has a good seven inches on them at least, even without counting the horns. But he's not gangly like a basketball player; he's built thick and muscular, and holy fuck, his cock is huge. No, *huge* isn't the right word. Did I say his thighs were *ruinous*? What a joke. His cock is the very definition of the word.

Even with the flicker of fear that curls through me, I can't stop myself from reaching out and dragging a single finger up, up, up his absurd length. "You're going to kill me with this."

He huffs out a strained laugh. "Baby girl, I've seen your toys. You can handle it."

I jolt, but I can't begin to say if it's from the pet name or the reminder that he has, in fact, seen me take a toy nearly this size. I'd completely forgotten about that, a little long-distance session we had a few years back. He'd purchased the toy for me, and I sent him a video of me using it.

I stroke his cock again, tracing one particularly prominent vein. Aside from sheer size, he's a familiar enough shape—give or take some delightful ridges—and he's got a wicked curve that makes my pussy pulse. "Any surprises here?"

"Not in the way you mean." He drinks me in with his gaze and then shakes his head sharply. "But I'm forgetting something." Azazel shoves off the bed and stalks naked to a cabinet against the wall. It's impossible to take my attention from him, the long lines of muscles in his back, his round ass, the flex of his thighs and calves as he walks. Gods, he's powerful to the point of beauty.

He returns, ridged cock a promise I am eager to fulfill, and dangles a pendant necklace before me. "This will ensure you don't get pregnant."

I blink. "I have an IUD."

"I'm aware." He doesn't move. "But I don't have evidence that science will hold up in our realm with magic in play, so we will be doubly sure that you're protected."

Warmth threatens to bloom in my chest. "You could just

wear a condom." He always has before with me—one of my nonnegotiable rules for clients.

"I could," he agrees easily. His attention drops to my pussy. "But I want to fill you up, baby girl." He leans down and plants a hand next to my hip, his rugged face intense. "Don't you want Daddy to make a mess of you?"

I can't breathe. My mouth works, but it takes several tries before I can dredge up an actual response. "You know I only call you Daddy to piss you off."

"I know." He grins suddenly. "But I've decided I like it."

I like it too. A lot. I'm stuck here for who knows how long, so it's not as if my situation can get *more* complicated. The logic is as flimsy as a butterfly's wings, but I don't care. "How does the pendant work?"

He presses it into my palm. "A single drop of blood will key it to you. As long as you're wearing it, it will prevent pregnancy with no side effects."

No side effects sounds kind of nice. I nibble my bottom lip. I came to him for frenzy, but it's hard to hold this kind of thing against him. Captor or not, he's taking care of me in his own way.

I am dangerously close to softening for him.

To avoid thinking about that, I drape the pendant around my neck and take his hand. I press a single finger to one of his claws. The bright bloom of blood against my skin makes us both draw in a harsh breath.

"The center," he murmurs, holding the pendant so I can smear my blood there. "A few drops of blood now and on the first day of your cycle."

I shiver and lift my gaze to his. "I'm ready, Daddy. Make a mess of me."

CHAPTER 10

AZAZEL

I know better than to accept what Eve offers me. She was almost taken from me today. She's only here because she's traumatized from the events of the day even though her life hasn't been exempt from violence. If Brosh's people had escaped with her, she wouldn't have survived the night.

The thought has me pressing her back onto my bed and running my hand down the center of her body. The bruise on her ribs is already fading; it will be gone by morning. It's the only evidence of what happened earlier, and yet I can't stop myself from touching her wide hips, her thick thighs, sure that there's some other injury I haven't catalogued yet. "They tried to take you from me."

Her eyes flash. "I'm not yours for someone to take."

If only that were true. If only I'd had enough self-control to stay away from this woman who intrigued me from the moment her sorrow drew me to her. Bargainers have a nose for people who may be receptive to a deal. Years ago, roughly six months before she met Pope and everything changed for her, Eve was one of those people.

If I'd properly approached her then, if I'd offered her a contract...

"You're mine now, Eve." I palm her pussy, soft and sweet and already wet for me. "You have been since long before you signed my contract."

She hisses out a breath that makes her breasts bounce. "It's in your best interest to stop talking and *fuck me*." She grabs my wrist and holds my hand to her heat. Some of the venom slips out of her tone. "Please, Azazel. I can't fight with you about this right now."

Is this harm? I'm not entirely sure, and that should be answer enough. I know what I would tell another bargainer in this situation, but I can't seem to take my own advice. I've compromised my ethics again and again when it comes to Eve. Why not now as well?

I can make her feel good. I can make her forget, at least for a little while. She came to *me* for this. I won't turn her away. I'll give her exactly what she wants, even if it damns us both.

So I stop thinking. I lean down over her and kiss her roughly. Eve tastes like she always has. Like home. If I ever had to define what that means, I don't know if I could put it into words. Maybe it's better that I don't.

She rises to meet me instantly, every bit of fight going into the slide of her tongue against mine, into the sharp pain of her teeth against my lower lip. She believes I've spent years lying to her, but the only untruth I've told is related to being human. All the rest was naked honesty. *This* is honest.

I drag my mouth over her jaw and down her throat. Her breasts are pure artistry, round and perfect and peaked with rosy nipples. I lavish one with a kiss while cupping them together and allowing my thumb claw to form so I can drag it along the lower curve of the other.

Eve whimpers. "Yes, Daddy. More."

Daddy.

If she ever fully comprehends what that name does for me when she moans it . . . Well, best not to think about that too closely. I would love to spend hours teasing her until she's shaking and desperate, but she won't tolerate that right now. She needs fast and hard and rough, to settle her in her skin.

I understand. It's what I need too.

Even so, I have no desire to hurt her, and if we move too fast, that's exactly what will happen. Pain has its place, but only so much of it. The balm can heal a lot, but I want her to enjoy this.

Any excuse to taste her again. Every time with Eve may be my last time; I'm too greedy for every detail, every sensation. I kiss my way down her rounded stomach, nibbling at the curve in a way that makes her squeak. I press my face to the apex of her thighs and inhale deeply. "I can't get enough of you."

"I . . ." She shudders out a breath as I push her thighs wide. "I don't know if I like you talking so much."

I use my thumbs to part her folds and flick her clit with my tongue. "Want me to stop?"

"I want you to *hurry up*." She reaches down to grab my horns, and it's my turn to shudder. They're not particularly sensitive, but there's something about the way she wrenches my face closer to her, demanding pleasure, that sends a shiver down my spine and makes my cock so hard, it's a wonder I don't come on the spot.

She's already dripping for me. I inhale again, making us both wait a beat before I cover her with my mouth and kiss her pussy just the way she likes. Eve makes a mewling noise that I'll hear in my dreams for the rest of my life. "Oh, fuck."

Just as her thighs tighten on either side of my head, she jerks my horns with each shiver and shake. I push one finger into her. My hands are bigger in my true form. Everything is bigger in my true form. I have to get her ready for me. I need to . . .

"Azazel." Her heels dig into my back. "Daddy, please. I don't want to wait anymore." She jerks on my horns again. "Fuck me."

I press my forehead to her lower stomach. "I'm going to hurt you."

"Then hurt me," she moans. "I can take it."

I wedge a second finger into her. It's a tight fit, her pussy pulsing around me. "Eve—"

"Then let me be on top."

I pump my fingers slowly into her, stretching her even as she soaks me to the wrist. "You came to me."

"And now I want to come *on* you." She gasps. "Azazel, please. That feels so good."

I want the same thing she wants. I can't pretend I don't. "You'll go slow," I murmur against her heated flesh. "Promise me."

"I promise, Daddy."

After one last long lick, I shift us around so that I'm on my back on the bed and she's straddling my hips. Her color is high, pink splayed across her chest. Her nipples are still glistening from my mouth. Her pussy . . .

Eve wraps her hand around my cock as best she can and shivers. "I can't wait to have you inside me." She shifts forward so my cock is pinned between us, rubbing herself along my length. Wet and hot and *gods.*

I grab her hips. "If you don't stop doing that, I'm going to come too fast."

"That's never been an issue before." She doesn't stop. Of course she doesn't. My woman has more than a little bit of a sadistic streak. Instead, she grinds down harder and draws her finger through the pre-come I can't contain. "Is this all for me?"

"I have a lot more for you," I grit out.

"Good." She has to arrange herself in a squat to rise enough to press the head of my cock to her entrance. I maintain my hold on her as she wiggles, working her way down over the head of my cock. "Damn," Eve breathes.

"Slow."

"Fuck off." She laughs, the sound ragged and almost mean. It makes my balls draw up. She's never been mean to me before. Not when I was a client. I hadn't realized how much I'd like it. It feels honest in a way I don't know how to describe. Eve rolls her hips, working her way down my length in fits and starts.

The urge to slam her down to the hilt is nearly overwhelming, but I'm too busy trying not to orgasm before she has a chance to take me all the way. Letting her be on top was a mistake. She's too sexy, panting and whimpering as she works to take me. Her belly shakes with each jerk of her hips, and I want to grab her, bite her, mark her as mine in any way she'll allow. It feels like frenzy, but I'm tense and still.

Seeing my cock spread her pussy, stretch her, get slick with her need . . .

I should close my eyes, but I can't tear my gaze away. "You're so fucking beautiful, baby girl."

"I know." She doesn't quite pull off her smirk, because her eyes are rolling back in her head. One last roll of her hips, and we're sealed together. I press a hand to her stomach, to squeeze her there, and she whimpers. "Fuck, that feels so good, Daddy. You're so big."

"You take me so well," I murmur. I stroke her clit lightly with my thumb. "You're close."

"Yes," she moans. She tilts her head back, exposing the long line of her neck, and starts to ride me.

"I can tell. Now be a good girl and make yourself come on my cock."

Each slow roll of her hips has pleasure building. She's a fucking vision, sweat slicking her skin, her expression dreamy as she chases her own orgasm. As she *uses me* to do it. It's degrading in the best way possible. I'm a tool for my queen, and fuck if it doesn't get me off knowing that she came to *me* when she was in need.

No matter what else is true for the two of us, Eve trusts me on some level. We can build something from that foundation, no matter how thoroughly I've fucked up handling this process.

The first flutters start, and then she's crying out, grinding down hard as she orgasms. *"Azazel."* My name on her lips is barely more than a whisper, but it's the most beautiful thing I've ever heard.

I can't hold out any longer. I dig my heels into the bed and thrust up into her. I'm not so far gone as to be rough with her, but I'm not as gentle as I want to be. I grip her hips and bounce her on my cock, again and again, and then I'm coming in great spurts, filling her and then overfilling her, my seed sliding down her thighs and all over my lap.

I sit up and pull her close. Eve shivers in my arms, her eyes still closed. "Fuck, Daddy, I think you broke me."

"You did so well," I murmur against her temple while I stroke her spine. "You were perfect." I'm still half-hard inside her, but she can't take me again. She needs something else right now.

I reach over without looking and dig through my nightstand until I come up with the balm I keep there. It's good for a number of uses—like healing the bruise on her ribs—but it was created a very long time ago by a witch who took one of my people for a lover. The size difference can be a boon, but she wasn't a fan of the soreness that prevented her from having her lover as often as she craved.

Eve winces as I ease her off my cock. Her eyes flutter open. "Fuck, maybe you really did break me."

"I'll make it better." I lay her down on my bed and take a moment to soak in every detail. The way her skin glistens. Her pussy, a complete mess from my cock. Best of all, her relaxed expression. None of the tension that rode her so strongly remains in evidence.

I mean to keep it that way.

She frowns a little when I kneel between her thighs. "I don't think I can take anymore. I'm going to be feeling you for a week."

"Trust me." I dip a single finger into the balm, coating it fully, and then press it into her.

She winces again, but the healing takes hold almost immediately. Eve's frown eases, and she shakes her head slowly. "Oh. That's good. That's really good."

"I think you've got one more in you, baby girl. I mean to have it."

CHAPTER 11

EVE

*F*ucking Azazel is something I'm going to curse myself for in the morning, but I can't seem to worry about it right now. No matter how different he looks, he's still *my* Azazel in bed. We're still getting off on the exchange in power that doesn't have a defined set of rules beyond what feels good in the moment.

And now, kneeling between my thighs with his cock still dripping, he fingers me back to full health. Magic is a hell of a drug, that's for damn sure. He's being careful with me, but he's not about to let me out of his bed before he gets *another one* from me.

He strokes his finger over my G-spot, his expression a mask of concentration all devoted to my pleasure.

The pain of taking someone his size is already fading, need taking hold once more. It consumes me, ensuring there's no space for thinking, for fear, for worrying about the future. There's only the here and now, Azazel's thick finger inside me, lazily building my desire.

Another one, indeed.

Azazel adds his thumb to the mix, dragging it over my clit

with each stroke. My first orgasm was damn near violent. This one feels almost like comfort, a gentle wave cresting and sending me back to the shore. It feels like *safety*.

He slows his strokes, eases his big finger out of me, and leans down to press a light kiss to my lips. "Don't move."

As if I could. I lie there and watch him pad naked to a doorway that obviously leads into his bathroom. He returns a minute later with a damp washcloth.

Even with the balm having chased away the worst side effects of taking him so recklessly, I still ache a little when he presses the cloth to my pussy. His onyx eyes miss nothing. "The balm will continue to work. You shouldn't be sore at all in an hour or so."

"Okay."

He frowns but finishes cleaning me up and tosses the cloth into a short bin I hadn't noticed before. "Stay."

I shouldn't. I'm already feeling vulnerable and raw in a way that has nothing to do with my body. He protected me today. He didn't hesitate to give me exactly what I asked for—what I needed—when I came knocking at his door at an indecent hour. More than that, he's submitted to my anger, to my punishments, without complaint.

He lied to me. Tricked me. Essentially kidnapped me. He . . . *chose* me. That shouldn't matter—I didn't ask for this—but it does.

I'm softening. Damn it.

"I'll stay."

He doesn't ask if I'm sure. He's too smart for that. Instead, he gets me a glass of water, watches closely as I drink it, shows me where everything is in the bathroom, and when I'm finished there, bundles me up in a blanket and sprawls us out in his bed.

It *should* be uncomfortable. I don't sleep with clients, and I haven't dated anyone in a truly spectacular amount of time. But the moment I close my eyes, Azazel's steady breathing relaxes every tense part of me as his warmth cocoons me in safety.

It's a lie.

The voice is faint, toothless. I'll work to get my barriers up tomorrow . . . maybe.

But when I wake up, it's to an empty bed.

I blink a few times, wondering if I imagined the whole thing. The faint ache in my body gives lie to that thought immediately. I sit up slowly, my head spinning faintly. "How long did I sleep?" Even knowing it's foolish, I can't help calling, "Azazel?" Silence is the only response.

There's no reason for the spike of hurt that realization brings. I've spent every moment since I arrived here pushing him away. Why should I expect he'd give me the courtesy of at least writing a note or something to greet me when I woke?

But I *am* hurt.

I climb off the bed and look around. His room is a larger version of mine, the color scheme dark—deep-blue walls, copper accents on the furniture, all of which is some kind of black wood I don't recognize. The temptation rises to snoop, but my bruised pride . . . bruised *heart* . . . can't stand the thought of being here a moment longer.

"I'm overreacting." The words feel faint and insecure in a way that makes my skin crawl.

Azazel is not my boyfriend. He's my captor. Just because we're fucking, just because he demonstrates care when he's with me, does not change that fact. I know Stockholm Syndrome doesn't exist exactly, but if it did, the sheer power of the orgasms he gives me would be enough to scramble my brain.

I shove through the door and out into the hall. I almost snap a command but force myself to pause and moderate my tone. "I'd like to go back to my room. Please."

With every step I take down the long hallway, I berate myself for my recklessness, for letting pheromones and hormones make me forget exactly what brought me here in the first place. For . . . a lot of things.

Homesickness rises, so strong that I press my hand to my chest as if I can soothe the feeling with touch alone. It doesn't help. Of course it doesn't help. I don't even know what I'm homesick for. My empty apartment? New York? Pope and the few friends I've allowed myself over the years? The clients who will just move on to other professionals once they realize I'm no longer around? I may have built up the fantasy that I'm irreplaceable, but it's not the truth. That realization hurts almost as much as Azazel's betrayal.

I'm in a magical realm a million lifetimes from everything I know, and I can't stop jumping on my captor's cock. I'm giving him exactly what he wants. It's easier to be angry with Azazel than to examine all the ways I feel hurt and foolish right now.

The first corner brings me back to my door. "Thank you." I can't quite make my tone be gracious. I shove through my door and head directly to the bathroom. I'm going to shower and then . . .

The rest of my life stretches out before me, with me lonely and alienated. I've been here over a week. That's barely enough time to adjust, but trying to explore feels like giving in. I wrap my arms around myself, more conflicted than I've ever been. I don't know what to do. I don't know what to *feel.*

Showering does nothing to clear my mind. Getting ready usually creates a calm space inside me, the motions familiar and comforting. Not today. I give up halfway through and march out to the wardrobe to pull on a black wrap dress. It's beautiful and fits perfectly, which only worsens my mood.

I have to get out of here.

Even if that means seeing him before I'm ready. This room is massive, but the walls feel like they're closing in. I have to go . . . I need to . . .

I push through the door. "Please." It's getting easier to talk to the castle, feels less like I'm talking to myself. Or maybe desperation has a way of cleaving through things that don't matter. "I need to get out. Just for a little while. I need . . ."

Walking helps keep the buzzing feeling that's beneath my skin at bay, but only barely. It's so much worse than it was last night, but I'll throw myself out a window before I beg the castle to send me to Azazel.

No matter how much I crave the feeling of his strong arms around me. That craving is a lie, a weakness. Giving in to it will only pave the way for him to get what he wants. He ruined my life.

He saved my life.

Only because he's the one who endangered it!

Fuck, now I'm arguing with myself. This is bad.

I turn two corners and nearly weep at the sight of a staircase opening up in front of me. "Thank you." I rush forward, moving too quickly, but I can't seem to slow down. The voices in my head are drowned out by two words, repeated over and over again until they bleed into each other.

Get out. Get out. Get out. Getoutgetoutgetoutgetout.

I'm moving so fast, I trip over my feet. For a moment, I'm perfectly weightless, and then I crash into a body. It catches me around the waist and keeps me from landing on my face. "Eve? What's wrong?"

Ramanu.

I *know* that the sensation of my ribs cracking, of my sternum splitting, of my heart emerging, bloody and frantic, is panic. It's not real. It can't possibly be real. But though my brain knows that, my body hasn't gotten the memo. "Can't. Breathe."

To their credit, Ramanu doesn't hesitate. They loop an arm around my waist and turn smoothly to keep walking in the direction I was headed. "You're safe."

"No."

"You are," they insist. Calm and steady. Their tone isn't

patronizing or pitying. Just matter-of-fact. "You're having a panic attack." We round another corner. "I'm taking you to the gardens. We're almost there."

They half carry me the rest of the way. My legs aren't quite working the way I need them to be. *Nothing* is working the way I need it to. Can someone die from panic? Surely that's possible. Rabbits die from fear, right? Why wouldn't it be possible for humans too?

Ramanu hauls me through a wide doorway, and then the sun is on my face, warm and buttery and as gentle as the caress of a mother I've never met. They bring me to a low bench and urge me down. "Here, darling." They guide my arms up to cross over my chest, my hands to the front of each shoulder. Then they tap their fingers over mine, back and forth, back and forth. "Breathe. Focus on the sensation." Back and forth. "Again. There you go."

My eyes burn. "I can't—"

"You can." They speak firmly and softly, still tapping in that regular rhythm. "Give it time."

I don't know how long it goes on for. It feels like a small eternity. I can't even say when I finally manage to draw a full breath or when the horrible tightness in my chest eases, just a little. Only that it happens. Eventually.

Through it all, Ramanu crouches before me, as patient as a saint, talking to me softly as they continue tapping. Them having horns where most humans have eyes turns out to be comforting. They squeeze my shoulders. "Better?"

"A little." I clear my throat. "Sorry. I didn't mean to lose it."

"You've been through a lot." They rise and sit on the bench next to me. "Do you want to talk about it?"

And have whatever I say go directly back to Azazel? I think not. I clear my throat and drop my arms. "I'd like to go into the city. The walls are feeling too close in the castle."

"That's not an option after yesterday." To their credit, they say it regretfully. "Azazel has ordered a lockdown until he can investigate further." They motion to the garden. "There are plenty of open-air places within the castle. This garden is midsized, but there are others."

For the first time, I look around the space, taking in the splashes of greenery and bright blooms. I'm no horticulturist, but even if I were, I suspect I wouldn't be able to identify these strange plants and flowers. They're beautiful, though. Now that I'm able to focus on something beyond breathing, I can practically *taste* the life in the air.

That doesn't make this less of a cage.

"Ramanu—"

Their head jerks up, their attention focused on something far away as tension bleeds into their lean body. "I'm sorry, Eve, but I have to go." They stand abruptly. "Azazel would like you to attend dinner with him tonight."

Before I can dredge up a rejection of *that* idea, they're rushing across the garden and through the doorway. I squint. For a moment, it looked like they'd actually disappeared, rather than just left. I want to say that's impossible, but that's what I thought about demons and magic and a host of other things I've encountered in the last week.

I slump back onto the bench. I can't remember the last time I had a panic attack. I must have been a teenager. They were something I dealt with in junior high and high school. They started after the foster family—the one I thought I'd be with forever—adopted a baby and suddenly had no room or space for my troubled preteen self. The next home wasn't bad, but there were four kids there and never enough attention to go around. Getting lost in the shuffle made me feel unmoored, and that sensation gave way to panic. It's been years—decades— since the last attack. Long enough for time to dull the memory, to remove some of its teeth.

My heart is still beating too fast, my muscles as shaky as if

I'd just completed an intense workout. I'm exhausted, but the thought of going back to my room is too much to bear. Instead, I make myself stand and walk through the garden.

As Ramanu said, it's not particularly large—roughly the size of my penthouse back home—but whoever designed it was clever. The greenery is explosive. The paths are narrow and winding. I take several circuitous routes before the buzzing in my brain finally retreats enough for me to think. Mostly.

Not only am I trapped in this realm, but now I'm trapped in the castle. How long before Azazel gets high-handed and decides the only safe place for me is my bedroom? Or *his* bedroom?

The fizzle of lust that rises in response to the thought only serves to piss me the fuck off. Yes, I came to him last night when I didn't know where else to go. Yes, he gave me what I thought I needed. But that doesn't change the fact that it's manipulation. We don't have equal power in this . . . whatever the fuck it is . . . if he can restrict my movements and cut me off even further from the outside world.

And then he summons me to dinner like an errant child.

I stop, narrowing my eyes. Fine. I'll attend dinner. But I'm going to make him choke on my presence.

CHAPTER 12

AZAZEL

"*R*usalka is here."

I look up from the report that I've been staring blankly at for . . . a period of time. I'm not sure how long. "What?"

Ramanu drops into the chair across from my desk. "She brought Belladonna for a shopping trip. They both seem content, but there was no warning for this visit, so I'm not sure if you want to look into it or not."

I do. Ramanu is keeping an eye on the humans who were sent with the other territory leaders, and while some of them are doing better than others, Belladonna is the one I'm most concerned about. She was raised in a toxic religious household and has internalized a number of falsehoods as a result. The god her people worship is nothing like the ones mine do; he's controlling and cruel and determined to flog his followers into submission. I hate seeing the pain it causes, the scars. Her coming from that background means she can't be entirely trusted to advocate for herself. That's why I spoke with Rusalka ahead of the meeting to ensure Belladonna went back to their realm, instead of with one of the others. "I'll invite them to stay for dinner."

Ramanu winces. "Yeah, about that."

"Why do you have that look on your face?"

Instead of answering directly, they frown. "What happened last night after the attack? Eve seemed shaky, but mostly okay. There was nothing in her emotions to indicate she'd end up in a spiral that resulted in a particularly nasty panic attack this morning."

I go still. "A panic attack?"

"It's a good thing the castle sent me to her," Ramanu says slowly. I can actually feel their attention narrowing on me. "I don't like the idea of her suffering through that alone."

Alone. Suffering.

Because I was too damn cowardly to face her waking up, knowing she'd regret everything that happened between us. I have no illusions about the wrongs I've committed against her. I deserve her anger. But I care about Eve, and every time she comes to me for sex while holding so much anger, it hurts. It's a hurt I'll shoulder until the end of time, but I'm only mortal. Sometimes I need to retreat.

I just didn't expect my retreat to cause Eve more pain. "What was wrong?"

"You didn't answer my question." Ramanu's tone gains an edge. "What happened last night? This morning?"

"It's none of your business."

"Wrong." They shake their head. "You may embody the over-protective-bargainer persona, but every single one of us has those same instincts. I didn't make the deal with Eve, but *you* decided to put her on that dais, which means she falls under my check-ins. So you will, in fact, answer my question, Azazel."

I have to concentrate on holding their gaze. That, more than anything, prompts me to answer honestly. "She came to me last night and wanted sex as comfort. She was a little rattled from the violence. She slept in my bed afterward." Each sentence is stilted.

"You bloody fool." Ramanu shakes their head. "Damn it, Azazel. You left her alone, didn't you? Fucked her sideways, cracked her right open emotionally, and then weren't there to catch her when she woke up feeling vulnerable."

I flinch. "I had work to do." The excuse feels as flimsy as mist.

"You're afraid."

I hold up a hand. "Stop reading my emotions."

Ramanu scoffs and slouches back into the chair, crossing one long leg over the other. "It's literally how I see, asshole. If you don't want to be perceived, learn how to shield better."

I have many skills, but shielding from Ramanu's sight isn't one of them. That doesn't mean it's comfortable to hear those truths stated so baldly. "Is she okay, Ramanu?"

"*Okay* is a relative term." They shrug. "She's angry and overwhelmed and hurt. She wasn't struggling to draw breath when I left her, but I would have preferred to stay with her longer. Unfortunately, Rusalka has poor timing."

It's tempting to rush to Eve and try to talk to her, but I'm still the leader of this territory, and there are a lot of people depending on me not fucking up relations with the rest of the realm. I'm on the best terms with Rusalka, and that needs to be honored. "I'll speak with Eve at dinner."

Ramanu's attention is like static against my skin. "You're too smart to act so foolish."

"I know." There's nothing else to say. Except . . . "I need Brosh found, Ramanu. I can't fix anything until the threat is truly eliminated."

"If you thought Brosh was the only threat, you would have eliminated him a long time ago."

I wish that were the truth. I sigh. "Family is complicated." And my family has been tangled up with the leadership of this territory since its founding. Most of them can see the benefit of what I'm doing, but . . . "If I go around murdering my cousins in cold blood, it will turn the entire family against me." If *that* happens, then dealing with Brosh will look like playground antics.

"I don't envy you the balancing act you're in the midst of." They hesitate. "The list of people I trust to handle this is smaller than I'd like."

I know. Most of my people are happy with the changes I've made. The trade alliances benefit our territory where war only ripped families apart and resulted in far too many of our young adults gone far too soon. We're longer-lived in this realm due to the magic inherent in every atom. It means those scars aren't going away anytime in the near future.

But there are always those who want more power, who flourished in the violence of war. Some of them are louder—like Brosh and his followers—than others. It's those that worry me. I might be willing to risk my own safety to build trust with those people, to bring them over to my way of thinking, but I would never willingly risk Eve's safety for the same.

"There has to be someone," I finally say. "You can oversee things, but with you leaving at any moment to chase your witch, it's too risky to have your attention split." Or to delay the search.

I have half a mind to command Ramanu to stay, to deal with their witch later, but that's not an acceptable command. They haven't made a bargain in ages, and the amount of time they've spent watching the witch nearly rivals mine with Eve. It's important to them, and I'd be a shit leader if I prioritized my fear over their potential happiness.

They consider for long enough to make me restless, before finally saying, "I think Nuin and Ziven are safe options. Both have their reasons for preferring your leadership to someone like Brosh. They also have no direct connection with anyone in your family, which is a small miracle. They won't be conflicted if they find him."

"Talk to them and set up the search."

"Will do." Ramanu sighs. "Eve isn't going to play nice at dinner. You know that, right? She's going to put on a show for Rusalka and Belladonna."

I hate that they're right. I give a sigh of my own. "Well, maybe it will teach Belladonna a thing or two about advocating for herself."

Ramanu smirks and starts for the door. "Or maybe she'll see a kindred martyr when she looks at you." They waltz out of the room before I can work up a response to *that*.

* * *

DINNER STARTS to go wrong the moment I sit down. It's clear enough that Rusalka and Belladonna are getting along swimmingly. I made the right choice in sending her to them. That's small enough comfort when Eve sashays into the room, brimming with fury in a way I've never seen from her before.

She looks beautiful in her anger, dressed to kill in black, each step dripping acid and aimed directly at me.

I clear my throat as she downs half her wine in a single swallow. "This is Eve. Eve, this is Rusalka and Belladonna."

"I remember you." Eve looks at Belladonna, some of the tightness fading from her expression. "You were part of the auction."

"Yes." Belladonna leans forward, curiosity alighting her expression. There's none of the wounded woman whom I first made a deal with present, which would be more of a relief if I weren't so acutely aware of Eve's anger. Belladonna smiles. "It's been an interesting experience."

"Interesting. That's one way to put it." Eve downs the rest of her glass. She's drinking too fast, as if she's fleeing something . . . or working up the destructive courage for a fight. I can feel Rusalka's eyes on me, but I can't pull my attention away from my woman.

At least until Belladonna crosses her arms over her chest, a small frown appearing between her brows. "You're not happy here."

"Ding, ding, ding." Eve raises her glass in a mock toast.

I grab the wine bottle before she can refill it. A lost cause as such things go; she just shrugs and grabs my glass instead. I try to catch her wrist, but she evades me and snags it.

Belladonna frowns harder. "If you're being mistreated—"

"Mind your tongue," I growl. I'm still too focused on Eve to moderate my tone. A mistake.

"I don't care if you made the initial deal that got her here," Rusalka snaps. "If you use that tone again, I'll rip out *your* tongue."

Eve laughs bitterly. "Down, *Daddy*." She turns to address Belladonna, and some of the venom in her tone eases. "Thank you for your concern, but I'm fine. I'm *safe*." She practically spits the word. "What reason do I have to be angry?"

All the reason in the world, and we both know it. I sigh. "Eve . . ."

"I think I've had enough. Good night." She rises unsteadily to her feet, sweeping up Belladonna's wine as she does, and wobbles out of the room.

I don't know where she's headed, but I can't let her go alone. I shove to my feet. "I apologize. This isn't how I'd hoped things would go. I have to see to Eve."

"Wait." The sharp command doesn't come from Rusalka, like I would expect. It comes from Belladonna.

I force myself to pause and give her my attention even though every instinct is demanding I charge out of the room. "Yes?"

She swallows visibly. "I know you said time moves differently, but . . . my sister?"

Frustration blooms like a poison flower inside me. I have to work to lock down my expression. It's not Belladonna's fault that her family is awful to the point that I'm tempted to wipe them off the face of the earth. She made the deal to save her sister, and I'd be a monster to shove my anger at *this* woman, who's looking at me with hope in her eyes.

I swallow down another sigh. "She was gifted with an anonymous medical scholarship to cover her treatment the moment you signed the deal." I can't quite keep a sneer off my face. "Your parents believe it's a reward for her faith that your god would provide."

"Not my god. Not anymore." Belladonna shakes a little but nods. "Thank you for telling me."

"Of course." Later, I'll pause to consider the implication in her words, to allow myself to hope that her changed belief is true. Right now, I need to deal with Eve. "Stay as long as you like. One of my people will escort you to the portal when you're ready to go."

I move out of the room as quickly as I can without running. Despite it having only been a minute or two, Eve has made good progress. Or at least she started that way. As I close in on her location, she weaves drunkenly to the wall and uses her hands to "walk" along it.

"You're acting ridiculous," I snarl. I sweep her into my arms without missing a step, ignoring her cursing protest. "You can barely walk, so I'll carry you."

"I hate you." She swallows the dregs of Belladonna's wine and drops the cup to bounce along on the floor behind us. Three glasses would be enough to knock her on her ass if they were stretched out over the course of an evening. To have downed them in less than fifteen minutes means she's well on her way to passing out.

"I'm aware," I snap. Even as I speak, I curse myself for letting my frustration take hold. She has every right to be angry with me. Just because I love Eve doesn't mean I'm entitled to a single thing from her.

The effects of the alcohol continue to sweep over her as I climb the stairs toward her room. Her body goes loose, and her head lolls against my chest. "You weren't there," she whispers.

I almost miss a step. I don't have to ask what she means. I already know. "I didn't think you'd want me there."

"Liar. Again. Even though you said you'd stop." She wags a finger in front of my face, her words slurring dangerously. "You felt it too." Her eyes drift closed. "I know you . . ."

I frown down at her. "Eve?"

No answer. I stop short, suddenly sure that she's dead. A foolish, irrational thought. She drank enough to get drunk, but nowhere near enough to be truly dangerous. Even so, when I reach the landing at the top of the stairs, I hesitate before finally saying, "My room."

The castle makes me work for it. Apparently it's angry at me too.

By the time it allows me to reach my room, I'm too exhausted to worry about the implications of bringing her to my bed instead of her own. I could pretend it's to ensure she stays safe through the night, but the truth is much more vulnerable.

I want her close to me. No matter the consequences.

CHAPTER 13

EVE

I thought waking up in Azazel's bed alone was the worst feeling. I was wrong. Waking up next to him is. The hangover doesn't help—my head is filled with throbbing razor blades—but it's the steady sound of his breathing that has me fighting not to scramble away.

Maybe it would have been less horrible if he were touching me, if I could explain away my reaction as anything other than emotional. Instead, he's a perfectly polite distance away, stretched out on his stomach, his face tucked against the bend of his arm. What little I can see of his expression is perfectly relaxed.

He looks like an entirely different person.

The temptation to reach out and run my hand over his muscular back is nearly overwhelming. That way lies danger, and I want to pretend I'm too wary to fall into the trap of caring for him, but yesterday more than proves me a liar.

It would be so easy to simply . . . give in. To let his presence seduce me as thoroughly as his touch has. To let him protect me, cage me, set me up in this new life so far from my normal one. To be whisked away by him *choosing* me. That's how magnetic he is, how much I still want him despite my anger.

"You're staring," he says without opening his eyes.

The urge to bolt from the bed rises, but I can't quite work up the energy. I roll onto my side and pull his soft comforter up to my chin. The move reminds me that I'm still wearing the dress from last night, which is absolutely absurd. Azazel has had his mouth all over every inch of me, but he apparently drew the line at changing my clothing while I was drunk and passing out. I don't want that realization to make me like him more. I truly don't.

"Why?"

He cracks open one eye. "Why what?"

"Why has Brosh decided that killing *me* is the answer? If he doesn't like how things are going in the territory, why not try to take it for himself?" Asking the question is dangerous. I'm already buckling for him without understanding his motives. I still want to know.

He's quiet for long enough that I think he won't answer. Finally, Azazel sighs. "For the same reason I haven't killed him—even if I could find him. He's my cousin. No matter how much he hates me, if he kills me in cold blood, he'll turn the majority of our family—and we have extensive numbers in very powerful positions—against him. He's not confident he can take me in a duel, so instead he's going after you to hurt me."

I blink. Of all the explanations, *family* didn't even occur to me. "But what is so bad about what you're doing that he wants to hurt you so desperately? Your people seem happy enough."

"It comes down to power. The result of the people of this realm mingling with humans a long time again was children who possessed significantly more magic than their nonhuman parents. My realm is one of magic. It's in every breath you inhale, the food you eat, the ground beneath your feet. But the strength of each territory, drawn into place so long ago that no one remembers how our ancestors did it, comes directly from the strength of the leader. The more magic the territory leader has, the more their people benefit."

What he's saying sounds like something out of a storybook, but I'm long past the point of disbelief. "I'm following you so far."

"When the realms split, that intermingling stopped. The only people who could jump to your realm were bargainers, and even then, only the most powerful could do it regularly. As generations passed, the magic in the other territories in this realm has faltered. It's not gone, but it's significantly decreased . . . while the bargainer territory has remained strong."

Easy enough to draw conclusions from there. "So you've been the most powerful for a long time." My mind jumps ahead, considering how he just handed over four human women to the leaders of other territories. "Why would you threaten your power like that?"

"Because I'm tired." He exhales heavily. "Apologies, that's a pat answer. The more complicated one is that war only benefits a small number of people—at the cost of far too many lives. We've been at a tentative peace since I took over, but resources aren't as plentiful as they used to be. The other leaders are strong in their own ways, but they need an avenue forward to help their people. By helping them help their territories, I pave the way to long-lasting peace."

I snort. "Or you do until one of them—or their descendants —gets power hungry and starts the whole process again."

He sighs again. "Yes. Though I don't think that's a risk with the current leadership. Sol—the dragon—is honorable enough to make my teeth ache. The kraken, Thane, is still grieving the loss of his husband, but he will do what's right for his people. Bram . . ." His gaze goes distant. "Well, I'm worried about Bram, but there's little enough I can do in the meantime. And Rusalka is probably the best leader in this realm. They'll take care of their territory—and Belladonna too."

Belladonna. The woman at dinner last night. I have to admit that she seemed happy. Genuinely happy. It boggles my mind a bit, but then, Rusalka didn't spend years lying to her about their identity.

The reminder sits heavy in my chest. I sit up. "So your cousin wants to keep the power isolated with the bargainers instead of sharing it."

"To put it simply, yes."

Damn Azazel for making me respect his ideals, even if they've resulted in endangering me. His people aren't my people —no one in this realm is—but I'm not so coldhearted as to say they don't matter. It doesn't make what I've lost easier to bear, though. It just makes me understand him a little bit more.

I sit up. "Why me? Why go through this intricate song and dance for so long?"

Another long silence. This time I wait. I need to know the answer.

"There was a moment in your life," he finally says. "Less than six months before you met Pope."

I frown. "What about it?" I don't like thinking about how dark the place I occupied during that time was, how hard it was, how low I got before Pope walked into my life and changed everything.

"Part of having bargainers' magic is being drawn to the humans most susceptible to making deals. I was going to approach you then, but you met Pope before I decided the best avenue to meet you." He doesn't look at me. "Becoming your client was supposed to be my in. But that first night . . ."

I remember. I don't want to, but I do. Azazel wasn't my first client, but he was the first one that made me forget myself, at least a little. He made me feel seen and valued in a way that I needed desperately. He walked into that room filled with other professionals, took one look at me, and chose *me*. And then he kept coming back for me—and only me—through the years. It felt special. It made *me* feel special. "What about that night?"

He carefully rolls onto his side and looks up at me. "You were figuring it out. You didn't need a bargain. You had it handled."

Okay, that's not where I thought that was going. "So you just decided to lurk in my life and wait for me to hit rock bottom again?"

"No." He sits up. "Absolutely fucking not. I enjoyed spending time with you. I . . . didn't want to stop."

I don't know how to feel about everything he's told me. Maybe he's not a complete monster, hunting me across the years, but he's been selfish. He's lied to me. He put me in danger and didn't bother to find another solution before he used that danger to trick me into doing what he wanted all along— making a deal with him.

For all that . . .

I carefully climb out of the soft massive bed. "I'm going back to my room."

"Eve."

I don't want to look at him. I'm hanging by a thread here, and I can't begin to explain what happens if that thread snaps. "Yes?"

"I know it doesn't change anything, but I'm sorry. Truly."

The worst part is that I believe him. If his enemies hadn't decided to target me, maybe I would have spent the rest of my years as an escort enjoying the nights with him as a client. I don't know. I can't *think*.

But even as I open my mouth to tell him that this changes nothing, that I still hate him . . . I can't quite manage the words. They feel too much like a lie, and as angry as I still am, I can't meet his honesty this morning with lies meant to hurt him. I don't know where that leaves us. I don't know much of anything at all right now.

I say nothing as I walk to the door and step through it. Directly into my room. I blink, some of my confusion melting away in awe of the castle. "I didn't know you could do that," I say softly. "That's really cool."

My doorknob rattles, and I raise my brows. It's never done that before; maybe it's Azazel chasing me down, but I don't think so. I cautiously open the door, and my jaw drops at the sight of a garden. It's not the same as the space I broke down in yesterday. This one is massive, with large trees stretching so high, I can almost believe I'm truly outside. "It's so beautiful."

When I walked out of Azazel's room, I fully intended to head straight for the shower and maybe have a good cry over how conflicted I feel. Instead, I find myself stepping into this garden and breathing deeply.

Only to pause when I catch the scent of coffee.

I feel a little silly following my nose like some kind of cartoon character. The path winds through the trees and flowers and plants, a practical paradise, to a small courtyard with a table and a single chair in it. On the table is a covered plate, still steaming in the cool morning air, and a carafe of what appears to be coffee.

I look around, but no one appears. "Is this for me?" The trees rustle around me as if in affirmation. I smile. "Thank you."

As I pull out the chair, I almost expect someone to approach and tell me that I'm stealing their breakfast, but the courtyard stays as quiet and soothing as it was the moment I arrived.

The first sip of coffee is divine. I haven't been hungover like this in a very long time. I like wine and the occasional whisky, but the older I get, the less it's worth overindulging. The hangovers seem to get longer and longer, while the drunk shenanigans become significantly less cute.

Lifting the plate cover reveals exactly the type of breakfast

I'm craving—fried eggs, hashbrowns, and crispy bacon. I stare down at it. "I didn't think you had food like what I'm used to here." Which isn't to say the food I've eaten since arriving here is bad. Quite the contrary. It's been delicious to the point where I resent it. But it's not familiar in the way this plate is.

I almost ask if it's a trick, but that seems unbearably rude. "Thank you."

The rustling of the trees is my only response.

* * *

OVER THE NEXT FEW DAYS, Azazel keeps a careful distance. I only see him for meals, and even then, he's distantly polite. Likely, he's feeling guilty all over again, and while I should find that satisfying, the truth is that I'm damned tired of this one-sided fighting.

I still can't bring myself to forgive him for trapping me here, though.

Despite my determination to do . . . something . . . I find myself returning to the garden the castle showed me, again and again. The castle provides any number of things in an attempt to keep me occupied. Books written in a language I don't understand, because apparently the spell Azazel placed on me without my permission doesn't extend to reading. A sketchbook and watercolors that I toy with, more out of boredom than any true artistic desire or ability. And, finally, a basket filled with skeined yarn in a variety of colors and weights, along with needles in a range of sizes.

And so I pick up knitting again. Pope bullied me into learning the skill few years back; he claimed it would be good for my mental health to keep my hands busy. They were right— they usually are—and it became an activity I gravitated toward again and again over the years. I don't exactly set out to knit a sweater, but I start a pattern I've knit enough times that I mostly have it memorized. I've never had use for so many knitted garments, so I always donated the final pieces to a nearby women's shelter. I don't know what I'll do with *this* sweater, but the familiarity of knitting it is comforting, especially when the castle somehow pipes through soft music to keep me company.

When I'm here, I can almost pretend that I'm free. It's a bandage, and not even a good one at that, but it's something. It soothes my anger.

At least until I look up one morning to realize I'm not alone. Azazel stands a respectful distance away, his hands clasped behind his back. He's wearing his "work" clothing—a long tunic that's split up the sides nearly to his hips, paired with pants and boots.

I freeze, suddenly feeling vulnerable and defensive. "What are you doing here?"

"I came looking for you." He glances around as if he's never seen this place before. "I haven't been in this garden in years. I forgot it existed."

"Or maybe the castle didn't want to remind you."

He smiles briefly. "There's that as well." Azazel clears his throat. "If you're up for it, I thought we could get out of the castle for a little while?"

"The prisoner gets a furlough. How lovely."

He opens his mouth, no doubt to tell me that I'm not a prisoner, before seeming to change his mind. "If you don't want to leave, you're more than welcome to say no."

I glare, because he's got me over a barrel and he knows it. No matter how lovely the garden, how eager the castle is to entertain me, it's all still a cage. Getting a chance to leave it, even temporarily, isn't something I'm going to pass on. I set my knitting aside, tucking it carefully back into the basket, and rise. "Where are we going?"

He's cautious—I'll give him that. He doesn't smile or react at all, other than to motion for me to walk next to him. "Ramanu is gone for a time. Some of their responsibilities have been handed off to others, but I need to make an appearance at one of the local villages just outside the city."

I fall into step next to Azazel, trying not to notice how he shortens his stride to match mine instead of making me chase him. "Where is Ramanu?" I haven't seen them in a couple of days, but I just assumed they were making the rounds, checking on the humans with the other territory leaders.

"There's a witch they've had their eye on—so to speak—for some time. She's finally gotten around to summoning them, so they've gone to offer her a bargain."

I swallow down an acid comment about the phrasing of them making a bargain instead of kidnapping their mark. If we start fighting, it will end in me storming off, and I'll miss my chance to get out of the castle for a bit.

Azazel, of course, divines the direction of my thoughts. "I'm not proud of the way I lied to you, but don't take that as a sign of how bargains are typically struck. If Ramanu's witch agrees, it will be on her own terms and because she wants to."

For the first time since coming here, I'm forced to wonder what I would have done if Azazel had come to me with honesty instead of lies. Would I have shut him down? Or would I have seriously considered his offer?

It bothers me that I don't know the answer to that question.

CHAPTER 14

AZAZEL

*C*atching Eve unfurl the farther we get from the castle makes my chest hurt. I knew she was unhappy, but it's so easy to justify the cost when I'm not the one paying it. We could have portaled directly to the village in question, but I chose a spot about an hour's walk away. My reasons weren't entirely altruistic—I wanted more time with her—but now I'm even gladder I made that choice.

She walks down the wide dirt path with her head tilted back and her face to the sun. Today, she's wearing a loose shirt and a long skirt, looking just as beautiful as she always does.

"Tell me about this village," she says without looking over.

A nice, neutral topic. "The city takes up a decent portion of our territory, but there are dozens of villages in the surrounding area. Most of them have a heavy focus in agriculture and trade agreements with the city to sell whatever they produce that their community won't need. Those agreements are generous, which benefits both the city and the villages."

"Hmmm." She glances at me. "Who put those agreements into place?"

Heat spreads beneath my skin. I keep my gaze forward.

"There have been trade agreements since the founding of the territory."

"I'm sure. But not *these* agreements." Eve is still speaking as if feeling out her reasoning. "Are the terms of the agreement another thing Brosh is furious about?"

The heat in my skin gets more uncomfortable. "Without farming villages like the one we're visiting today, the city starves. We have plenty of stores saved up, and there are gardens within the city proper, so it wouldn't happen quickly, but eventually it *would* happen."

Eve laughs a little, the sound strained. "You didn't answer my question."

"Fine," I snap. "Yes, I changed the terms when I took over. It's shortsighted to rule by fear and even more shortsighted to take instead of paying fair prices. And they always took more than the villages could afford to lose. The moment communities start starving, the seed for violence takes root. Yes, the city pays through the nose for that food, but the amount is still less than we pay in trade agreements with other territories."

She doesn't say anything for several long minutes. The day is pleasant, warm without being hot, with just enough clouds in the sky to prevent the sun from feeling overbearing. I hardly notice it.

Especially when Eve sighs. "You know, you're making it very hard to hate you, Azazel."

I don't know what to say to that, what answer won't cause this strange moment between us to fracture. So I say nothing at all. I simply walk next to Eve and slowly, after a while, start pointing out the birds and small animals that flutter and scurry across our path. It's . . . nice.

I pause right before the path turns into the descent that will take us to the village. This is always the hard part for me. I lead because it's the right thing to do, because Caesarea was my aunt and so many other members of my family contributed to the harm done under her rule. I decided I didn't want to live in a world like the one they'd fostered. It would have been easy to say I wanted change and then sit back and do nothing, but that's not how I'm formed. I had power to change things, had support to make it happen, and so I did. The battle for my territory's people is one I'll be fighting for the rest of my life.

This part, though? There's a reason I delegated the village visits to Ramanu. I inhale slowly and exhale just as slowly. Then I do it again a few more times. I'm aware of Eve watching me, but she asks no questions, and I'm not in the mood to explain myself. Not about *this*.

It's so foolish. There's no reason to be so dramatic. Nothing bad is going to happen, and it won't kill me to be uncomfortable for a short period of time. "Let's go." I start walking again.

It takes no time at all to reach the village. As I expected—dreaded—there's a welcoming committee. My cousin Alice is first to reach us; she's a broad woman nearly as tall as I am, with curving horns and deep-purple skin. Her curly dark hair bounces with each step she takes, and her wide grin calms some of my nerves. "Old Man Azazel! It's about time you came around." She claps me on the shoulder hard enough that I have to brace myself not to stagger.

"Old Man Azazel," Eve murmurs.

Alice turns to Eve, her dark-brown eyes lighting up with interest. "So *you're* the human who has the old man in a tizzy." She grins wider. "Can't say I blame him. Look at you!"

To my shock, Eve's cheeks turn pink, and she stammers a little. "I, uh, I . . . I'm Eve."

"Pleasure." Alice takes Eve's hand and bends over it, then places a lingering kiss on her knuckles. I don't realize I'm growling until Alice gives me a cheeky grin and bounces to her feet. "I'm just playing. You know I'd never step on your toes like that. You're family, after all."

Eve sputters out a shocked laugh. "Did you just say *family*?"

"Alice is another one of my cousins." As the baby of the bunch, nearly thirty years younger than me, she's seemed to take it as her mission in life to loosen the rest of us up.

"That's right. Youngest of seven, gods bless my saintly mother." Alice loops her arm through Eve's and turns her easily to start heading deeper into the village.

Saintly mother is one way to put it. Alice's mother was the strong right hand of Caesarea. She was greatly favored to become the next leader, and although she wasn't as bad as Caesarea, she had facilitated the monster's actions and policies. Fear of that, more than anything, is what made me challenge our leader for the position.

I don't like to think of that battle. I don't like to think about how it cost me half my family, how it created a divide that I'm not sure will ever be resolved. Before. After. The old way. The new.

Alice doesn't seem to hold any of it against me, but I still feel awkward whenever I'm required to come out here and interact with her and her people. She leads us to the village square, which currently contains three massive tables piled high with food.

She catches me looking and grins. "Come now, old man. I know this was supposed to be a generic check-in on the community, but you never come out this way these days. I had to make an event of it."

Of course she did.

I open my mouth to remind my cousin that we're not staying long, but the words stall in my throat when I catch sight of Eve's interest as she takes in the sight before us. This may be a little slice of torment for me, but I can endure it if it will make her happy. "Alice, give us a moment."

She shrugs. "Sure thing. I'm going to see about the band."

Gods preserve me, I truly hope she did not say what I think she just said. I watch her walk away and veer from one gathered small group to the next, an easy word ready for every single one of her people. Alice may be young by our people's standards, but she's a natural leader, and her village has flourished since she took over.

Eve turns to me, a smile pulling at the edges of her lips. "You two could not be more different."

"I'm aware." No reason to resent Alice for putting the woman I love at ease when all I manage to do is hurt her. I strive to push down my irritation. "We don't have to stay long. I just need to do the rounds."

"Do the rounds," she murmurs. "Tour the fields? Maybe kiss some babies?"

I'm flushing again. "Something like that."

"Azazel . . ." She glances at the people gathered. "Could we stay? Just for a little while? It should be safe, right?"

I wouldn't have brought her with me if I wasn't sure that Alice ran a tight ship and held a deep hatred for Brosh and all of his ilk. "It's safe enough."

She surveys me. "But this makes you deeply uncomfortable. Why?"

If anyone else had asked, I would beg off answering the question. But this is Eve, and while we may hardly have a relationship as such things go, the least I can do is answer whatever question she chooses to ask me. At least she's speaking to me at all. "I don't think I should be praised for doing the right thing."

Eve seems to digest that. She turns her attention to where Alice laughs with a group of children, each holding a ribbon attached to a stick. My cousin truly went all out for this ambush. Finally, Eve says, "There's praise and there's appreciation. If it makes you that uncomfortable, why didn't you send someone else out today? Surely there are other people beyond Ramanu who can do this."

"Two reasons: It may make me deeply uncomfortable to go through this song and dance, but it makes them happy, and I would have to be a monster to stomp on that." It's an effort not to shuffle my feet. "And I wanted an excuse to spend time with you. I knew you would say yes to leaving the castle."

Instead of telling me she hates me again, her smile widens, blooming from a faint curve to something more real. "If you really want to leave, we can."

I sigh. "No, we can't. You don't want to. And it would hurt Alice's feelings."

Her grin reaches her eyes. "Yep."

"That's a neat little trap you set for me to walk into."

She actually laughs. Not a bitter chuckle. Not a choked, angry sound. A true laugh, loud and boisterous, tossing her head back. "You're high-handed and aggravating, but you have a soft, gooey center, don't you?" She leans in, her amusement drawing me close even though I know better than to believe this might truly be a turning point for us. Eve lowers her voice, practically purring. "Poor Daddy. Being perceived is deeply uncomfortable, isn't it?"

All the blood in my body rushes south. I tense. Fuck staying here. If she's going to speak to me in *that* tone of voice, I'm going to toss her over my shoulder and haul her gorgeous ass to the nearest clearing to fuck her within an inch of her life. Every thought in my head goes to how lovely she looks with lust flushing her body, how perfect her pussy is when she's taking my cock, in . . .

Except Eve is walking away from me, a swing in her step, her skirt swishing as she glances over her shoulder and winks at me. *The little brat.*

I have to turn away, have to take deep breaths and focus on the sound of my cousin's voice braying with laughter behind me in order to get my body under control again. It takes a bare minute, but by the time I turn around again, Eve is in the midst of the villagers, chatting easily and smiling as if she's having a great time.

"I like her."

I jolt. I hadn't noticed Alice closing the distance. "I do too."

My cousin loops her arm through mine. "Let's get the tour out of the way. Be prepared to ooh and aah over our fields!" She seems to notice that my steps are slow and raises her brows. "I know you've had some trouble, but she's safe here. Every single one of my people would toss themselves on a sword for you, and *we* don't undervalue the humans who are in our territory."

There are only half a dozen or so currently in this village, two of whom are linked to Alice through contracts. "I know." It's still hard to walk away from Eve—and that has little to do with the ever-present danger and more to do with the fact she was *flirting* with me. Not in order to escape. Not out of spite. She teased me just because she could. How can I see that as anything but progress?

True to her word, Alice keeps the tour of the nearby fields short. It's an effort to stay focused, but I'm here for a reason. I frown as we finish with the last one and turn back toward the village proper. "You've expanded quite a bit since last year."

"We have." She shrugs. "The land is doing well, and our numbers have grown. We gained three new families in the last six months alone. Not everyone is cut out for city life; they've slipped right into our rhythm without much friction at all."

"Will you need supplemental help come harvest time?"

She chuckles. "We always need supplemental help during harvest time."

I don't know how leadership sits so easily on her shoulders. I suspect it has to do with a difference in personalities. From the moment she was born, Alice has moved through the world in a completely different way than I do. "I'll make sure to put the word out. There are plenty of young adults who can afford to spend a season with you. The city will supplement their wages, of course."

"Of course," Alice says dryly. "It's not necessary, though. We can afford the cost. Our coffers are full, thanks to your trading policies."

"That's why I said *supplement*." I nudge her with my shoulder. "You have a lot to take pride in here, Alice. You've done a good job. But the city is prosperous enough to help, and so it should."

She's silent nearly all the way back, only speaking when she pulls me to a stop as we reach the first house. "You're doing good work, Azazel. I know it's a thankless task to run this territory, especially with so many of the old guard rumbling about the changes, but the changes *are* good. So many people who were barely getting by before are prospering. That's important."

I clear my throat. "Uh, thanks."

"Yes, yes, I'll stop praising you now." She shakes her head and moves forward again. "I hear the music starting up. You'd better make sure you dance with your girl." She shoots a grin over her shoulder. "Otherwise, I might beat you to the chance."

CHAPTER 15

EVE

*O*nce, Pope took the lot of us to some kind of harvest festival, and we had one hell of a good time with the spiked cider and apple picking. This is a lot like that . . . and also not.

It seems like the entire village has come out in celebration. There's a four-person band striking up a tune. The food smells amazing. Children dart through the gathered people, giggling and shouting with glee. Teenagers make eyes at one another from their respective friend groups. This isn't a party with an eye for tourists; this is for this community, a social event that it seems like everyone pitched in to make happen. Now they get to enjoy the fruits of their labor.

"Eve."

Two couples begin to dance. Then three. Then four. The people gathered quickly move back to create an open space for them to spin one another around. My heart lurches at the joy on the dancers' faces.

"Eve."

I can't quite tear my gaze away. Not even for Azazel. "What?"

"Would you like to dance?"

I know what I should say, but I can't quite dredge up the anger that's been brimming beneath my skin since the moment I woke up in this realm and realized what he'd done. It's not that I forgive him—I don't know what it will take to get there, or if it's even possible. It's more that I'm starting to fully understand the kind of man Azazel is . . . to recognize in him the client I shared meals and conversations with over the years. The stories he told me may have been edited, but they seem to hold a core truth.

Or maybe it's the call of the fiddle-like instrument one of the band members is playing, insistent and tempting. I don't know, but I set my hand in Azazel's and let him pull me onto the impromptu dance floor. I'm not short, but he's massive, and it feels a little absurd as he carefully places one hand on my waist.

Staring up at his roughly handsome face has my heart doing unforgivable things. I shiver at the naked *need* in his eyes as he leads me around the circle, picking up speed once I get the rhythm down. There don't seem to be specific steps, but we dance and dance until I'm dizzy and the whole world narrows to the man tethering me with a perfectly polite touch.

I can't stop myself from laughing in giddiness. It's worth it, because Azazel loses some of his intensity and grins down at me, relaxing for the first time in . . . I don't know. Ever, maybe?

"Ready for a spin?" He doesn't wait for me to reply before he changes his grip on my hand and sends me whirling before him. He catches my hip again, continuing to move with my momentum, as someone cheers in the background—Alice, I think.

As I'm dancing with Azazel, it's so easy to forget all the bad things that have happened. At least for a little while. The song changes and changes again, and neither of us flags or suggests a break. My breathing comes hard, sweat gathers along my spine, and my muscles ache from more use than I've given them since arriving here.

Except for the sex.

There's no use thinking about *that* right now. Not when every nerve ending feels alive and brimming with lightning. Not when Azazel's big hand is on my waist, his heart in his onyx eyes.

The music shifts. I glance over to find the drummer and the one playing a guitar-like instrument sitting back, sweat sheening their foreheads. They laugh and accept frothing mugs of beer, obviously ready to take a break. The fiddler turns the tune to something soft and achingly sweet.

We slow alongside the other dancers. Azazel clears his throat. "We can rest if you like."

"Not a chance." I laugh breathlessly. "I love to dance."

"I'm beginning to see the attraction." His fingers flex against my hip. "Eve—"

It's clear he's about to apologize again. I shake my head. "We don't have to talk about it again. I may not like what you did, but I'm beginning to understand why." I glance around. Everyone is so fucking *happy*. "What happens to orphans in this realm?" The question pops out before I have a chance to change my mind.

Azazel tenses slightly before seeming to make an attempt to relax into the gentle sway of our slow dance. "It's different in every territory, and even in mine, it varies. In most cases, a child would go to the nearest family member."

My throat feels thick. It's so silly. I've had a lifetime of therapy to work through the loss of my parents. I may have ended up in foster care, but I was one of the lucky ones. Though my first few sets of foster parents passed me on when they got what they really wanted—a baby—my final set weren't all that bad. Overstretched and drowning, they did their best with what they had. They never hurt their kids. The bare minimum, but better than some of the stories I've heard over the years. Getting

handed a check and a backpack when I graduated hurt—a lot—
but so many people have had it worse.

I don't know what Azazel reads in my expression. He does
me a kindness and continues. "In villages like this, if there's no
family, everyone comes together and decides who is best
prepared to take the child—or children. Then the village does
what it can to supplement things so that isn't a burden on the
primary caregiver."

"Is this one of the other things you supplement?"

He glances down. "Yes."

Of course it is. Because Azazel cares about his people and
uses his power to help them on multiple levels. "What about the
city?"

"We have specific families and programs that help them." He
meets my gaze steadily. "On its surface, it's not dissimilar to the
foster care system in your world, but those families are all
supported—and monitored—on multiple levels. In the villages,
everyone will intervene if something goes awry. In the city, it's
more formal. I won't pretend that every family is perfect or that
there haven't been bad things that happened, but we work hard
to ensure the children are protected."

The awful feeling in my throat gets worse. "That sounds like
it's too good to be true."

"It's not a perfect system. In a perfect system, there would be
no need for foster families." He clears his throat. "But there are
fewer children who are in need of parents or guardians now
than there were when we were constantly at war."

Damn him. I swallow hard. "You're making it *really* hard to
hate you."

He smiles wanly. "I'm sorry." Azazel turns us and moves
away from the dancing, though he keeps a hold on my hand.
"Let's get you something to eat and drink."

The moment we reach the table, he's mobbed. I nibble on a
cake that manages to be both savory and sweet and watch the

old folk pass Azazel around. He submits to their questions about when he'll get married and have children with faint laughter and an easy diversion that says he's been through this song and dance plenty of times before. He even kisses a damn baby at one point, holding them easily in his massive hands. I refuse to acknowledge the lurch in my stomach at the sight.

He may not be fully comfortable in this setting, receiving this attention, but he's quite good at it. And they all clearly love him. Why wouldn't they? The changes he's enacted have positively benefited their lives, families, and communities.

It doesn't excuse the danger he's put me in . . . but I'm having a hard time holding on to my anger. This is so much bigger than me. Yes, I wouldn't be in this mess if he hadn't spent the last few years as one of my best clients, but . . . It's not as if I didn't enjoy the time with him. It's not as if I didn't encourage him to keep booking me, to keep choosing me above the other professionals, even though I knew we were in danger of crossing several of my lines. If I'd told him to leave me alone, he would have.

But I didn't want him to go.

Alice plops down next to me, an easy grin on her face. "You know, I thought it was one-sided, but you're gone for him too, aren't you?" She ignores my shocked expression and keeps chatting in that deceptively casual tone. "Don't bother to deny it. You're sitting here watching him like you're seeing the next fifty, seventy, hundred years stretch out before you and you don't hate the idea of it."

I blink. "I'm thirty-five. There's no way I'll live another hundred years."

"You will if you stay here. It has something to do with the magic infused in every bit of our realm. It makes people live longer. And yes, it does apply to humans. Not everyone who makes a deal goes home at the end of their seven years."

Seven years. Not a lifetime.

My anger tries to bloom again, but it sputters and sparks,

not gaining momentum. I'm so damn tired of fighting. I don't know what that means for my future, but Azazel isn't a monster. He's a man who's made mistakes.

"I'll keep that in mind," I finally say.

Alice takes a long drink of her beer. "He's getting close to his limit. I'll distract them, and you get him out of here."

I glance at her in surprise. She's been boisterous and irreverent this whole time, but I should have realized there's a keen and caring mind under all that attitude. "I can do that."

"Good girl." Alice bounces to her feet and moves toward the band. A new song begins, and she lifts her mug over her head. "To Azazel!"

"To Azazel!" the crowd cheers. They flock to Alice, cheering and dancing.

The man himself appears at my side a moment later, looking a little hunted. "How are you holding up?"

"Come on." I take his hand. "Let's get out of here." Within seconds, we've slipped away. The sounds of celebration follow us into the trees and then finally fade to silence as we keep walking, putting distance between us and the village.

It's only when we've been accompanied by what I assume are the normal night sounds of the trees—it's not as if I have much experience with nature—that Azazel slows his stride and squeezes my hand. "Sorry about that. I didn't expect a full event. I should have, knowing Alice."

"It was fun."

He pauses and gives me a look. "You don't have to say that."

"I know." I find myself squeezing his hand back. "But it's the truth. You dance well."

"So do you."

This is awkward but not in a painful way. Almost like we're just meeting, just feeling each other out. It's strange, especially considering I know what he sounds like when he comes.

Azazel loosens his grip like he might drop my hand, but I

give him another squeeze and lace my fingers through his. "They love you."

"They don't know me." He shrugs. "Well, Alice does, but she's family. It's not the same."

My heart twinges, but I'm too content for it to be more than a passing ache. "I wouldn't know."

He gives me a sharp look. "Family isn't only blood. Pope knows you better than anyone."

My body flushes hot and then cold. "I'm aware." I swallow hard. I've been very pointedly not thinking about Pope too often, but they slip into my thoughts more and more as time goes on. "I miss them."

"I know. I'm sorry." He doesn't look at me. "After I deal with Brosh, I'll take you home. It never should have gotten this out of control. I never should have panicked. The thought of you being hurt . . ." Azazel gives himself a shake and drops my hand. "I wasn't thinking clearly. I was only reacting."

I could call him a liar, could ask him how long it took him to write up that contract and if that counted as solely *reacting*. I don't. It would hurt for the sake of hurting, and this moment feels as fragile as a soap bubble. "Azazel?"

"Yes?"

There are so many things I could say right now. The possibilities choke me. Today has shown me a different side of Azazel, but one that's so intimately familiar, reminding me I've known him for years. In the back of my mind, I've spent this entire time trying to reconcile the man I thought I knew and the monster who tricked and then kidnapped me. Today gave me both. They're the same. Facets of a single gem, priceless beyond measure.

I inhale deeply and stop. Azazel takes a few more steps before he realizes I'm not keeping pace. He turns to face me. "Eve?"

I close the distance between us slowly. "I don't know if I'll ever forgive you."

His expression goes tormented even as his gaze heats. "I know."

"But I'm . . ." I take another deep breath and press my hands to his chest. This feels scarier than anything I've experienced thus far, and that includes the attack the other day. "No matter how hard I try, I can't stop myself from caring."

"Eve," he breathes. "You don't have to."

But I've started and now I can't stop. "I don't know what it means for the future or for us or for anything, but I'm so damn tired of fighting. I just want . . ."

He waits. It seems like he barely breathes, like he'd stand right here and be content to listen to me falter my way through this for years.

"I just want you," I finish in a whisper.

Finally—*finally*—Azazel moves. He catches my hips and pulls me flush with his body. "Stay with me tonight?"

There's only one answer. There's only ever been one answer. "Yes."

I don't know how we get back to the castle. It feels like a fever dream of kisses and stumbling steps and questing hands that never quite reach where we need them. Between one step and the next, the forest fades away to be replaced by stone walls and then a familiar scent.

The castle took us to my garden.

Azazel strokes a hand down my spine and looks around. "We could—"

"I don't want to wait any more." I shove at his shirt. "Please, Azazel."

He lifts his arms, but he has to lower the rest of his body so I can get the tunic over his head. I toss it to the ground and go for his pants. He catches my wrists. "Eve—"

"If I don't get your cock in my mouth *right now*, I'm going to lose it."

He blinks. For a moment, I think he might argue, but he finally releases my wrists. "You don't have to."

"I'm aware." I slide his pants down his hips, freeing his thick cock. I love oral sex, both giving and receiving, and there's been a distinct lack of the former in my life. "Now be a good Daddy and try not to come too fast and ruin my fun."

CHAPTER 16

AZAZEL

*B*efore this moment, I would have said there's little Eve could ask of me that I wouldn't all but kill myself to give her. But this? I stand there, every muscle tense, as she wraps her fist around my cock and, with an impish smile, flicks her tongue over my slit. She's barely touched me and I'm fighting not to lose it.

I didn't expect her feelings to change. Why would they? She has every right to hate me, and if I'm going to spend the rest of my life loving her, I know better than to expect something in return.

But today was . . . nice. Exhausting, yes, but those kinds of visits always are. Dancing with Eve, though? Having moments where it almost felt like we were different people in simpler circumstances? It was better than I dared hope—if I had even thought to hope.

"Daddy." Eve squeezes my cock, her expression going wicked. "Normally when I'm between your thighs, you're not focused on anything but me."

"Sorry, baby girl." I carefully lace my fingers through her

hair. It's longer than she usually wears it, nearly to her shoulders. "I'm here."

"You will be." She doesn't give me a chance to respond, taking my cock in her mouth and sucking me down as if she never needs to breathe.

We've been in this exact position before, but never when in my true form. I should have expected it to be different, but up until this moment, with Eve's cheeks hollowed and her stroking her tongue along the underside of my length, I hadn't allowed myself to even imagine it.

She cups my balls, squeezing gently and causing lightning to shoot up my spine. Then her gaze sharpens, and her nails prick my sensitive skin. The command is clear enough: eyes on her.

"Enjoying yourself, baby girl?" I murmur.

Eve hums a little and resumes fucking me with her mouth, slow slides with a hint of teeth. She knows exactly what I like, and she gives it to me with everything she's got. I'm too big for her to take fully, but that only adds to the experience—especially when she uses her hands to make up the difference.

I want this to last forever.

Unfortunately, my body has other ideas. I can't stop myself from thrusting into her mouth, just a little. She gags and hums again, shifting her grip to my hips, urging me to move, to do it again.

I curse. "Going to come if you don't slow down."

She doesn't slow down. Of course she doesn't. I thrust again, meeting her mouth, making her gag and tears trail from her eyes even as she keeps it up. I fight to not fist my hands in her hair, to not do anything to hurt her, even a little, and then I'm orgasming, grinding against her lips and teeth as I come down her throat.

Eve keeps sucking me until I pull her off my cock. "Fuck, baby girl." My knees feel like they've turned to liquid. I manage not to collapse, but only barely, as I sink to kneel in front of her.

She licks her lips, looking particularly pleased with herself. "I missed that. A lot."

"Me too." I cup her cheeks, use my thumbs to wipe away her tears, and then kiss her. Tasting myself on her tongue is overwhelming. I want this to mean something. I want her to promise things I have no business asking her to promise.

It takes a few moments to get my strength back, and then I tug Eve to her feet. "Come here." I pull her shirt off, and she seems to realize what I need, because she doesn't try to help me. She simply lets me undress her, and I trail kisses across her body as I do.

Part of me wants to take her to bed right here and now, but it's like she was made for this place, the carefully cultivated greenery thick around us, the cobblestones of the pathway beneath my knees. No wonder the castle brought her to this space specifically. No wonder she's obviously been spending so much time here.

I lift her easily and set her on the table. "Show me."

Eve understands immediately what I mean. As I take a step back, she spreads her thighs and skates a hand down her stomach to part her folds. She's so wet, she's dripping all over the table. Her color is high, and her smile is impish. "Like what you see, Daddy?"

I go to my knees once more, enjoying the bite of stone against them. "I see a godsdamned mess. Better clean you up." I part her pussy and drag my tongue up her center. She tastes so good. She always tastes so fucking amazing.

"Oh, fuck." Eve wraps her hands around my horns, letting her head fall back and eyes close. "I'm never going to get enough of your mouth." She moans. "Daddy, please."

I'm out of patience. There's never enough time. There wasn't before, when I was pretending to be human and measuring my time with her in hours. There isn't now, when I continue to constantly misstep around her. I want forever with this woman, the frenzied fucking and the lazy lovemaking, but I know better than to say as much.

I impatiently push a finger into her, and then two. "Don't want to hurt you," I mutter against her pussy.

"Azazel." She jerks my horns. "If you hurt me, you can kiss me better later."

I stand and grab her hips to pull her off the table, then spin her around to bend her over it. I stroke a rough hand down her spine. "Spread for me, baby girl."

She obeys immediately, moaning when I palm her pussy and resume fucking her with my fingers. She's ready enough that I won't harm her, but only barely. Eve rocks back onto my fingers. "Fuck me. Now!"

The table isn't tall enough to get her where I need her, so I lift her hips, taking her feet clean off the floor, and push into her. I have to work to get the head of my cock past her entrance. I pause, breathing hard. "You're still too fucking tight."

Eve wriggles her hips, though she has no leverage to do anything at all. "Then do something about it, Daddy."

I work my way into her in short strokes. Her body gives way to mine a little at a time, her wetness making everything smoother. My earlier orgasm grants me a little more control this time, but watching her ass jiggle threatens to undo me. "You take me so sweetly."

Eve pants and shakes. "Fuck me, Daddy."

"Eve." I lean down and nip her shoulder as I press all the way into her. "So fucking greedy."

"Yes," she moans. "You feel so good."

I'm rapidly losing the ability to speak. *Good* doesn't begin to cover it. This is bliss. This is beyond comprehension. This is *love*.

"Don't stop." Her head falls forward, baring the back of her neck.

I kiss her there as I fuck her slowly, withdrawing almost

completely and then thrusting forward again. "I won't stop. Not until you're coming for me." It takes me a few tries to find the exact angle that makes her whimper and shriek, but once I do, I don't let up. I want to feel my woman come around my cock. She may hate me in the morning, might hate me right fucking now, but she's begging me not to stop, so I'll be damned if I don't give her exactly what she needs.

And then she's orgasming, her pussy pulsing around my cock and dragging me right over the edge with her. I grind into her as I finish. Gods, I love this woman. Even in this moment, I know better than to say it, but the emotion rolls over me, so strong that I could weep from it.

Things are a bit of a blur after that. I carry Eve into my room, somehow manage a shower, and then we collapse in bed. I think that might be it for the night, but she turns in my arms and kisses my throat. "Azazel?"

I'm instantly hard at the needy tone in her voice. "Yeah, baby?"

She rubs my cock with the heel of her palm. "You promised to kiss me better if I was sore."

Fuck, the things she does to me with that bratty tone of voice. "You're tired," I murmur as I reach behind me for the balm. "You should be asleep."

"You're right." She squeezes just beneath the head of my cock. "I know just the thing to get me there."

I want to be able to simply enjoy this or even to pretend that this is how it could always be with me and Eve. Her in my bed. Sex and jokes and conversations and *us*. I know better.

Nothing has changed for her. She's been honest with me from the start, her anger completely understandable. She may very well not forgive me. But if this is all she'll allow me to give her, then this is exactly what I'll do. I tug her leg up over my hip. After dipping my finger into the balm, I press it into her. "How's this to start?"

She shivers in my arms. "Pretty solid. But I have a better idea."

Eve pushes on my shoulders, and I allow her to guide me onto my back. She nabs the balm and smears a generous amount on my cock. I freeze. "Eve, that's not how it's meant to be used." I have nothing to heal, but that doesn't stop the balm from trying. A tingling radiates through my cock, making me hard enough that it's painful. *Fuck.*

"I know." She grins. "But can't hurt to try." She tugs me up to sit and grinds against my length. "Unless you want me to stop?"

"You know I don't."

"Thought not." She positions my cock at her entrance and sinks onto me. It's easier this time, though she still has to work for it, wedging me deeper and deeper until I'm sheathed to the hilt. Eve's eyes flutter closed. "I was right. Your cock really is ruinous."

It's so damned hard to focus with her clenched tight around me. "Do you need to—"

She keeps talking right over me. "How am I supposed to fuck other people when I've had you like this, Daddy? How am I supposed to want to?" There's something in her tone, something soft and sweet and aching.

I cup her face. Maybe this is the most honest we'll ever be with each other. "Do you want to keep fucking other people?" She may be the only one for me, but I'm well aware that I wasn't her only client. A possessive part of me always ached knowing she'd be with others the way she was with me, but the thing that irked me the most was the fact that I was just another client to her. She was never truly mine, even if I was hers.

Eve's lower lip trembles before she firms it. "I don't know," she whispers. "I won't pretend I didn't enjoy my work, but it was . . . work."

I don't know what to say to that. Even if I did, now's hardly the right time for this conversation. I sit up and wrap my arms around her as she starts to ride me. No matter what else this time brings, I can't regret it, because she's here with me. At least for now. To chase the thoughts from my head, I kiss her. Better to lose myself in the moment, in her, than to worry about what comes next.

Eve doesn't pick up her pace. She slides her hands up my chest and grabs my horns, using the leverage to angle my head back and drag her mouth over my throat. "Azazel?" Her voice is a demand for more. "I'm almost there."

I grip her hips and guide her to grind harder, working her clit against my stomach. "I've got you."

She orgasms with my name on her lips, and my heart is a fool ten times over because it's certain this changes things, even as my brain knows better.

Some things can't be forgiven.

The only thing I can do is remove the threat and send her home, pausing on the way out to ensure she has enough money that she never has to work again if she doesn't want to. It will mean losing her forever—there's no world where she'd welcome me as a client still, even if I were willing to continue endangering her. The contract will have to be nullified, but while that process is uncomfortable and will drain my power for a time, it's a small price to pay. If I hadn't been so damned selfish, Eve never would have been in danger.

Maybe, if I'd been honest from the start, it wouldn't have come to this.

Eve reaches between my thighs to cup my balls. Her gaze is a little dazed, but she's clearly not stopping until I come too. "Get out of that head, Daddy. You're in my hands now."

She squeezes, and there's no holding back my orgasm. I forget myself enough to slam her down on my cock once, twice, four times, and then I'm spilling inside her.

Bargainers don't believe in an afterlife the way humans do. Our gods are great and unknowable beings who formed the realms and then moved on to do whatever gods do with eternity stretching behind and before them. When we die, we become one with that universe, and sometimes a soul will be pulled back for another chance, many lifetimes in the future.

But if I believed in the concept of heaven—whatever that looks like—then *this* would be it. Exhausted and spent, Eve relaxes in my arms, tracing abstract patterns on my chest.

She sighs and kisses the spot she was just stroking. "Azazel?"

"Mmmm."

"If you keep fucking me like that, I might not have any choice but to forgive you."

She means it as a joke, but I can't take it as such. Not when it's about *this*. I hug her closer and press a kiss to her forehead. "You'll always have a choice. If you ever do forgive me, then it will be in your own time, when your heart is ready. *If* your heart is ever ready." I want that time to come, but I'm not confident it ever will. Not with everything I've done.

Eve makes a face like she wants to argue but finally shakes her head. "No, you're right. I'm sorry. The sex is too good. It's making me silly."

I tip her chin up and kiss her slowly. "I like you silly."

"Yeah?" She nips my bottom lip. "Well, you know what to do."

"I do." I kiss her again.

There are many hours left until dawn. I plan to use every one of them.

CHAPTER 17

EVE

*T*he next three weeks pass in a blur of . . . happiness. Azazel stops keeping me locked up in my room and starts bringing me with him as he takes up Ramanu's duties. Not all the leaders of the villages we visit are as supportive of him as Alice is, but they clearly respect him and his policies. And his people *love* him.

We spend each night in his bed, fucking and cuddling and sleeping.

He even has me sit in on his meetings with Nuin and Ziven, where they give their reports on their efforts to locate and capture Brosh. I like them both quite a bit.

Nuin is shorter than me, with deep-purple skin and thin, straight horns like some antelopes. She's clever and serious, laying out each stage of their search systematically.

Ziven is her opposite in every way. Ne is tall and lanky, with skin nearly the same shade as Azazel's, curving horns, and a deep laugh that makes me smile no matter the situation. Ne seems to have plenty of experience with finding people who don't want to be found.

It's only a matter of time before they find Brosh and this all ends.

That's what I should want. Azazel has promised to send me home once the danger has passed, which is what I was fighting for from the moment I woke up here.

Even so . . . I find myself hoping that Nuin and Ziven take their time.

The next morning, I wake up to find Azazel standing by the desk in his room, drinking his coffee and reading through an intimidating stack of papers. He's usually up before I am, but after the disastrous moment the first morning I woke up in his room, he's always here when I finally manage to roll out of bed.

I walk over, then wrap my arms around him from behind while pressing a kiss to his spine. "Morning."

"Morning." He squeezes my hand. "I have to go farther afield this morning, and unfortunately, it's not safe for you to join me."

I straighten. It's on the tip of my tongue to protest, but I can't truly argue that he's being overprotective when he's been working hard to ensure I don't feel trapped. If he's laying down this boundary now, then there's a reason for it. Still . . . "Why?"

"I need to check in on the women with the other territory leaders. Ramanu was doing it regularly, but with them still gone, I prefer to handle this task myself."

That makes sense. In the weeks since I've been here, it's become increasingly clear how seriously bargainers take their contracts. They don't fuck around when it comes to *their* humans' safety. Since Azazel made the deals with these women, their safety is his responsibility.

I sigh dramatically. "I *suppose* I can find a way to entertain myself while you're out flitting about the realm."

He rises and gives me a quick kiss. "I promise not to be long. I have to leave now, though. I was just waiting for you to wake up."

It's sweet, but the warmth in my chest fades as he leaves the room. I take my time getting ready, as if that can stave off the reality of my situation.

Nothing's really changed. I may have found peace with Azazel, but the moment I'm alone, I can't quite forget the fact I'm trapped here. Maybe I'd feel differently if I knew exactly what I was doing when I signed that contract, if I went into this with open eyes instead of lies.

I wander about the castle, murmuring to it softly as I do. It hasn't tried to fuck with me once since showing me what I've come to think of as my garden, and sometimes it brings me to new rooms and wings and what I can only describe as secrets. I'm hoping for one of those to distract me while Azazel is gone.

But it's barely thirty minutes before tension rolls through the halls and I'm abruptly spit out into a new hallway between one step and the next. I spin around, squinting. "You've never done *that* before." My stomach sloshes a little, but it's clear the castle wants me to go somewhere.

The floor heaves under my feet, tilting me forward, as if I could have possibly missed its intentions. I stumble. "Okay, okay, I'm going."

I hurry through the hall to the door at the end and shoulder it open . . . to find the petite redhead from the auction facing off with Azazel. In the few minutes I interacted with her that night, she seemed like the kind of woman who would rather flee than speak a harsh word to someone. Apparently a lot has changed in the last month.

I stand in the doorway, unseen by both of them, as they yell at each other. I can't quite divine what happened. Azazel says Briar was harmed and asks her if she wants medical care, but she seems intent on the fact that he's overstepping and misunderstood the situation.

Ramanu appears in the midst of it, and though I'm happy to see them, they have to grab Briar to stop her from jumping at Azazel. She tried to *attack* him. My jaw is on the floor, and even as my mind tells me to move, to step in, Ramanu muscles the yelling woman out of the room before I can manage to break free of my shock.

The entire thing takes bare minutes.

I give myself a shake and step into the doorway. "What's going on?"

Azazel looks up and meets my gaze. "I can explain."

That's exactly the *wrong* thing to say. I might have been able to set aside the situation I ended up in because it had only happened to me. Except . . . apparently that wasn't true. If Briar is this furious . . . If Azazel looks like he's already about to apologize . . . I take a step back. "What did you do?"

"Sol became . . . overzealous . . . and removed Briar's birth control pendant without prior discussion. He's forfeited his territory as a result."

I blink. Removing the birth control pendant without talking about it first is kind of a big deal. Except, I can't get Briar's fury out of my head. I would never tell someone who's a victim how they have to respond, but she was protesting in a way that makes me think he read the situation wrong. "From what she says, that's not the full story." It was hard to get the full context with how short and angry the fight was, but clearly Briar was angry at *Azazel*, not Sol.

He bristles visibly. "Not you too."

It's amazing how quickly the peace of the last three weeks melts away, leaving only anger. I stare up at him, my heart crumbling in my chest. "Because no one knows better than the great Azazel, right?"

His brows slam down. "That's not what I said."

"You didn't have to say it." I shake my head. "Your actions speak louder than whatever defense you're currently trying to come up with." Because there's always a defense. He might apologize, might take responsibility later, but in the moment, he uses whatever justification necessary to do what he wants.

He scrubs a hand over his head. "Eve, please."

Please. As if I'm the one being ridiculous right now. "I need time to think." I turn around and walk away. He's learned enough not to follow me, not to chase me down and battle his way forward.

The moment I turn the corner, I whisper, "Take me to her, please."

A few more turns, a few flights of stairs—as if the castle is truly testing whether I want this—and I'm deposited before a door nearly identical to the room I haven't bothered to visit in weeks.

I almost turn around right then and there. It's been *so nice* letting myself enjoy Azazel. With a little more time, I may have even convinced myself to let down the last of my barriers, to fall for him for real.

Or to admit to myself that I already have.

That, more than anything, makes me lift my hand to knock on the door. I'm not a person who turns away from hard truths, even if they threaten the little bubble I've allowed myself to be wrapped up in.

The door clicks open but not because anyone is on the other side. The castle again. I glance around. "Thank you."

The redhead—Briar—is sitting on the bed, her head in her hands. She straightens as I step into the room, her angry expression fading to one of confusion. "You . . ."

"Eve." I press my hand to my chest. "Sorry to intrude."

"No." She shakes her head, tear tracks on her pretty face. "It's probably best I'm not alone right now. I was just about to start trying to break down the door." She eyes it with suspicion. "It was locked just a minute ago."

"The castle has a strange sense of humor sometimes." I ease the door shut behind me, confident that I'm not about to be locked in again. The castle and I have an understanding, one that feels independent of Azazel.

Something to consider later.

"The castle. Right." Briar frowns. "I guess I do remember some of that from when I was here before." She shakes her head. "Regardless, I need Azazel to stop and listen to me. He walked into a conversation that was none of his business and took things out of context. Sol would *never* put me in danger intentionally. Yes, we didn't exactly have a conversation about the birth control pendant before he bit it off, but if I hadn't wanted him to do it, he wouldn't have done it."

The passion in her voice makes my heart ache. "You sound like you love him."

Briar gives me a wobbly smile. "He's the best man I've ever known."

And Azazel just dropped a bomb on their relationship, so to speak. *High-handed* doesn't begin to cover it. It's impossible to avoid comparing myself to Briar, even though the situation *is* different. The current danger against her sounds like it was perceived instead of real. Regardless, Azazel didn't stop to ask questions or find another way. He just took her . . . like he took me.

We chat for a little while. I came here to find out answers, and it quickly becomes clear that Briar truly is in love with Sol. They had a bit of a rocky start, because of the trauma from her past relationship and his awkward nobility, but it seems like things are going swimmingly now.

At least until Azazel ruined it all.

I don't know how to feel. I truly don't. It's not a simple situation, and I can't pretend that my time with him *hasn't* changed things for me, at least a little.

I'm not a coward, though. As tempting as it is to retreat to my room to clear my head, that would be a shitty way to go about navigating this. So I don't. I go to his.

He appears in the doorway a few minutes after me. I don't know if that's intentional on his part or if the castle had its way with him, but he doesn't immediately approach me. The distance can be measured in feet, but it feels like he might as well be standing on another planet. I cross my arms over my chest. "You fucked up."

"I disagree." His face gives me nothing. "She just needs time to understand."

I flinch. That's not what I expected him to say. I should have. "Like *I* needed time to understand? Because Daddy Azazel knows best?" I laugh harshly. "Right. Of course. Why would I assume you've learned anything at all? What's your motivation to change? All you had to do was wait me out and I fell for you, legs spread."

"Don't." He takes a step toward me. "Don't do that, Eve. That's not what this is. That's not what *we* are."

"Isn't it?" I whisper.

It's suddenly all too much. I skirt around him to the bathroom and make quick work of getting ready for bed. He doesn't say a word as he does the same. Or when we strip down and climb into bed. Or when he wraps a cautious arm around my waist and tugs me back into the curve of his body.

"I love you, Eve."

My chest feels too tight. *I love you too.* I don't say it aloud. I *can't* say it aloud. I wish hearing those words from him were enough to ward off the dread churning through my stomach.

CHAPTER 18

AZAZEL

I'm not surprised when Sol arrives in my castle three days later. To be fully truthful, I'm relieved. Eve's been spending every free moment with Briar, and with each hour that passes, I can feel the space between us growing. While I understand that fixing the problem with Briar and Sol won't fix the one between Eve and me, it can't hurt. Right?

I stare at the exhausted dragon standing in my office and resign myself to a stressful day. "Shut the door." I glare before he has a chance to speak. "If you start roaring, I will kick you out of here so fast, you might not survive the portal out."

Historically, Sol has been the most even-tempered of the other territory leaders. There's none of that present. He has to visibly wrestle his anger and worry under control before he can speak. "Is Briar okay?"

As if I would ever hurt her. But I decide to throw him a small kindness, no matter how little he deserves it after that stunt with her birth control pendant. "That little hellcat nearly took my face off."

He freezes. He doesn't seem to even breathe. "What?"

"You heard me."

"I did, but . . ." I understand his confusion. I suspect Briar has never come at *him* the way she came at me that first day back in the castle. He shakes his head sharply. "You've made a mistake."

"That's what she keeps saying." I press my claws to my temples, suddenly tired of it all. I just want to see Eve. I just want to figure out how to fix what I've broken. "Sit down."

Sol shifts a little, then finally sinks into the chair in front of my desk. When he speaks, he's managed to moderate his tone to sound more like himself. "When I signed my particular contract with you, I thought then that it made perfect sense. You wanted to expand the bargainer demon territory." The words are slow. His dark eyes see far too much.

Ah well. They were going to figure it out eventually. "You have something to say. Say it."

"I had some time to think while traveling. Several years ago, you said you wanted peace between the territories. I didn't believe you. None of us did."

He's almost there. I give him a long look. "I fail to see what influence your belief—or lack thereof—has to do with me or our current circumstances."

"It made sense that you'd set up a spiderweb with four neat little traps that will put you in charge of the entire realm. I didn't question it." He leans forward. "But you don't want my territory, do you? You don't want any of ours."

There it is. *Took you long enough.* "You wouldn't believe the gift without the strings attached. So I made them hefty ones." I shrug. "Even if I took all four territories, I wouldn't hold them indefinitely. Your respective peoples are too powerful and too stubborn. It's more trouble than it's worth."

Sol isn't particularly young, but he looks it right now. He's absolutely crestfallen. "Then why take Briar?"

"*That*, I was not fucking around with. I realize the rest of you think we keep the humans here as our playthings and see them as little more than toys to be used and discarded when the deals are up. That's not how it works. A contract is sacred."

He hesitates, then finally huffs out a breath. "I owe you an apology."

"I truly couldn't care less what you think of me." It's mostly true. "But you harmed one of mine, and *that* I will not forgive."

"Briar is not *yours*. She's *my* wife."

"Your wife *by my leave*."

The door swings open behind him, and he leaps out of my chair, fully expecting an attack. It's not one of *mine* slipping through the door. It's Briar, her hair pulled back into a complicated twist, wearing a deep-gray dress that looks absolutely devastating on her. I narrow my eyes. No doubt Eve is to credit for this timely appearance.

She catches sight of her husband and stops short. "Sol?"

"Briar." Gods, he's so in love with her that it makes me feel like a voyeur being in the same room as them.

She starts to move toward me, but I fling out a hand. "I swear to the gods, if you throw yourself into his arms right now, I will send you back to the human realm."

Briar spins on me and gives a truly impressive snarl. "You're so high-handed, it's no wonder Eve doesn't want you!"

I flinch. I can't help it. She's speaking words I know for truth, with such conviction that they would convince me even if I had doubts. I'm suddenly exhausted. It's clear these two love each other, and equally clear that Sol committed no harm against Briar. It takes a little while to get them out of my office and on their way home. It passes in a blur. All I can think of are Briar's words.

No wonder Eve doesn't want you.

I sit in my office for a long time after they leave, thinking of nothing at all. I love Eve. I've loved her for years, even as I resigned myself to always occupying a specific space in her life. Manipulating her into signing a contract was shitty. I could have explained the situation. Or I could have gone over her head to Pope and explained what they needed to know of the danger. They could have sent her into hiding.

I've been selfish and just as much an overbearing asshole as she's claimed.

I push to my feet with a sigh and go in search of my woman. Except she's not mine. She never will be. No matter what she feels for me—and I know Eve well enough at this point to understand that she does have feelings for me in some capacity —my deception will always stand between us and any future we could attempt.

For once, the castle is feeling kind. I only have to climb a single set of stairs before it spills me out into what I've come to consider Eve's Garden. She's here, knitting away at a blue garment. She's fast, needles clacking steadily even as her gaze is on something a million miles away. It's clearly a sweater, the fabric spilling over her lap. This mundane act of creation is a beautiful kind of magic as far as I'm concerned. I can't wait to see it finished.

If I do right by her, it never will be.

"Briar went home with Sol." When she doesn't immediately respond, I clear my throat. "I, uh, might have acted too hastily in that situation."

Her gaze flicks to my face, finally focusing on me, and there's such deep sadness there that I nearly hit my knees and beg for forgiveness. It won't make a difference. I've apologized, and she's rightly called me on the truth that I wouldn't do anything differently. She won't believe that my regret has taken hold enough for *this* apology to be true. I've given her no reason to.

Even so, I can't stop myself from moving closer. "I'll make things right."

Her lips twist. "Some things you can't make right, Azazel. No matter how hard you try." She finishes a row and carefully sets her knitting aside. "But I'm glad you saw reason when it comes to Briar and Sol. I think I'd like to meet him properly at some point. After hearing about him for the last few days, I feel like I know him."

My throat is so tight, I can barely get the words out. "I think Briar would welcome any chance to see you again." And then I *do* fall to my knees, because how can I not? "I'm sorry, Eve. Truly sorry."

She reaches out and cups my cheek. I would welcome her fury, her spite. Instead, she just smiles sadly. "I know you are." It feels like she's saying goodbye. She's touching me, but she's retreating all the same.

It makes me want to clasp her to me all the more, to hold her so tightly, she wouldn't dream of leaving. Which just proves I'm exactly the monster she believes me to be. I close my eyes. "With Ramanu back, we're closing in on Brosh."

"Azazel." She waits until I open my eyes to continue. "What difference does it make? I understand the situation well enough. If you kill or imprison him, it will just start a blood feud within your family. I won't be any safer then." She drops her hand and sits back. "You know, if you'd come to me with honesty, I probably would have signed the contract."

I stare. "No, you wouldn't have. You were happy in your life."

Her smile dims. "Not happy."

"Content, then. You've said before that you liked your job. You have Pope. You . . ."

Eve clears her throat. "You know I grew up in foster care." She continues before I have a chance to respond. "I was one of the privileged ones. Nothing *bad* ever happened to me." Her eyes shine in the fading light streaking through the trees around us. "But no one ever chose me."

I choose you.

I know better than to say it aloud. It's not the right time. She won't welcome it.

"That's part of what I like about the sex work. My clients choose me. They do more than choose me. They go out of their way to have me. They pay extravagant amounts of money, they beg Pope for the privilege, they do their best to ensure I never have cause to turn them away."

"Eve."

"So, yes, I like my job. I like the challenge of providing their perfect fantasy. I like the money—gods, I like the money. I love the freedom my life allows me. Or what it *allowed* me." Her lower lip quivers. "But what I really like—what I crave—is being chosen."

Gods, she's tearing my heart right out of my chest. "I'll make it right. I swear I will."

It's like she doesn't hear me. "You were my favorite. Did you know that? All those years ago, you picked me out of a lineup, and then afterward, you only wanted me." A single tear slips free. "I asked Pope, you know. If you were contracting any of the others. I was jealous." Her laugh is a little wet. "But you never did. You chose me that night and then you kept choosing me."

"I only ever wanted you," I whisper. I remember that first night. Pope is particular about their clientele and their people, and so they hosted an event. A trial run for both new clients and new sex workers on their staff. I had gone, sure that I saw my opportunity to make a deal with Eve slipping away. That's all that was supposed to happen that night. An offer.

Instead, I saw her standing in that line of people, proud and beautiful and a tiny bit unsure but trying not to show it. And I knew I wouldn't be offering a contract. I knew she was beyond me, but I wanted her in whatever way she'd allow. Becoming her client was the simplest and most honest way forward. Until I lied and ruined everything.

"I know." She wipes away her tear and visibly pulls herself together. "That's a heady thing, Azazel. So, yeah, if you'd come to me with a contract and an explanation . . . I might not have believed you at first, but I can't pretend I would have turned you away entirely."

"I'm sorry." I don't know what else to say. Bargainers may be able to jump realms, may be able to manipulate the timing of such jumps, but we can't actually time travel. I can't go back and do things differently. I can't fix anything.

"Me too."

CHAPTER 19

EVE

$\mathcal{I}$ lie in bed next to Azazel each night, tucked against his strong, warm body, only to wake up alone each morning. When we have sex, it's frenzied, as if each time is our last. We share meals, the conversation stilted and filled with things unsaid.

It feels like we're saying goodbye in slow motion. Truly, this time.

I love him, but how can I let myself sink fully into something that should be a joy when the circumstances make it a horror? I'm still trapped in the castle, still knitting away as if I'm the miller's daughter, trying to spin yarn into forgetting my reality. In the weeks that follow, I finish both sleeves of the sweater and complete the ribbing of the hem.

I'm weaving in the last end when the entire castle shudders. In my time here, we've never had anything resembling an earthquake, and from the way the floor suddenly angles beneath my feet, that's not what's happening now. "I'm going!"

The shaking continues as I hurry down the newly opened hallway and a single staircase. I nearly keep going, but the castle raises a step in front of me, stopping me in the doorway near the front entrance. I realize why immediately.

Azazel stands there, taking up even more space than he does normally. I thought I'd seen him furious before, but that was nothing compared to how lethal he sounds as he snarls, "What are you doing here?"

For a horrified moment, I almost convince myself he's talking to me, but he doesn't seem to even be aware that I'm close. Instead, he's glaring at . . . I shift a little to the side, trying to stay as much in the shadows as possible. *Oh.*

The bargainer in the doorway is nearly the same size as Azazel. The familial resemblance is uncanny: the same crimson skin, the same bald head with the same shape horns, the same massive body. The same ruggedly handsome face. The only difference is *this* bargainer's dark eyes are flat and furious. Brosh. It has to be.

He spreads his arms, arrogant and hateful. "I heard you were looking for me."

"Give me one good reason I shouldn't kill you where you stand."

"You're too honorable." Brosh says it like it's an insult. "Which is why you've taken us down a route we may never recover from as a people. That stops now." His grin is downright mean. "I challenge you for leadership of this territory."

I expect Azazel to curse him. Maybe to attack right here and now. He certainly looks like he wants to. Instead, he laughs in disbelief. "You bloody fool. You actually think you can beat me."

"I know I can."

Azazel shakes his head. "So be it. I accept. I'll have the square cleared within the hour. Get out of my sight until then."

Brosh backs up slowly, still smiling. "Best say goodbye to your little human. She won't survive to see nightfall."

I flinch. I can't help it. I've had some truly horrific experiences with exes, but I've never been threatened so casually—or intentionally. The doors slam shut in Brosh's face, then the lock clicks loudly in the sudden silence. It won't be enough to keep him out, not when Azazel has accepted his challenge.

Azazel has accepted his challenge.

"Don't do it." I step up and into the hallway, crossing to Azazel. "Don't fight him."

His brows go up when he sees me, but he doesn't chastise me for eavesdropping. He just pulls me into his arms, holds me close like he may not get another opportunity to do so. "This was always the plan, Eve."

Eve. Not baby girl.

There's no reason for that distinction to hurt, less reason for it to worry me even more. I cling to him and bury my face in his chest. "Please, Daddy. I can't stand the thought of something happening to you." We might be broken to a degree that there's no fixing, but I still love him. I don't want him hurt. I sure as fuck don't want him *dead*.

He strokes a hand up my spine and cups the back of my head. "You'll be safe as soon as he's dead. I intended to challenge him, but he's made things even simpler. *He* challenged *me*. No one in my family, my territory, or the entire damned realm can say it wasn't fairly done." He kisses my forehead and steps back. "And when he's dead, I'll nullify the contract and send you home. You have my word."

I stare up into his handsome face. This is what I wanted, isn't it? To be safe. To return home and regain my freedom. To get my life back.

So why does the idea of it feel so empty?

Azazel doesn't give me time to process. His attention snags on something behind me. "You heard."

Ramanu's voice sounds just as troubled as I feel. "I heard. You sure about this?"

"Yes."

Ramanu sighs. "Then I'd best get to work on getting the

square ready." They clear their throat. "Eve, I'd like to introduce you to Lenora. She's been here a little while, but you've been distracted and I didn't want to intrude."

Distracted. That's one way to put it. I make myself drop my arms and turn away from Azazel to find a pretty white woman standing next to Ramanu. She's got lightly tanned skin, long dark hair, and a sharply curious look on her face. "I've heard a lot about you."

"All good things, all good things." Though Ramanu is trying to put a good face on things, their tone is distracted and worried. "Keep an eye on her."

"Of course." Lenora accepts their distracted kiss and then they sweep away, slip through the doors and out of the castle. She raises an eyebrow at Azazel. "Don't you have some preparing to do? I have a spell or two that could come in handy if you're interested."

"That would be cheating."

There's the soft sound of movement behind me, and when I turn around, Azazel is gone. I can't help the way my shoulders drop at the realization. "What if he loses?"

"Then he dies, and Ramanu and I spirit you back to the human realm before that bastard Brosh has a chance to lay a single finger on you." She takes in my stricken expression and winces. "Right. Wrong priority. You're not worried about your freedom—you're worried about *him*."

"Of course I'm worried about him," I snap. It's not fair to take my fear and frustration out on this woman I just met, but I can't help it. "I love him."

"Hmm. Have you told him that?" She holds up her hands when I glare. "Guess not. I'd advise against any last-minute declarations of feelings until after he wins. That kind of thing gets distracting."

"You are *not helping*," I hiss.

"Right." Lenora shrugs. "Look, if Azazel is half as good as

Ramanu is, he'll have this in the bag. Did you know Ramanu ripped off my ex's head in a similar tournament battle? It was deeply impressive, even if the blood got everywhere."

I blink. Obviously I am aware of Ramanu's and Azazel's prowess as warriors. The fight in front of the castle all those weeks ago was proof enough of that. But while that experience traumatized the fuck out of me, apparently violence excites Lenora. She's practically vibrating as she recounts the battle, giving me entirely more detail than I need. By the end of it, I'm feeling woozy. "That's . . . something."

Her smile is sharp. "And it stopped you from freaking out about Azazel for a little while." She loops her arm through mine. "Come on. We may as well get a good seat."

I find myself digging in my heels. "It's not safe."

"Honey, it's about as safe as it can be. Brosh is confident enough to challenge Azazel, so he won't fuck with you in the meantime."

I don't know how this woman seems to have such a grasp on things when I'm spinning out, but maybe that's part of what drew Ramanu to her in the first place: She's entirely unbothered by this whole fiasco.

Truth be told, the thought of waiting in my room to find out if Azazel is dead or victorious is too much. I nod jerkily. "Okay, fine. Let's go."

To my surprise, the castle doesn't try to stop us. The doors open easily, and we march toward the square where Ramanu took me shopping on that ill-fated day. In the time Lenora was spinning her bloody tale, the center of the square has been entirely cleared and a crowd has gathered around the perimeter.

Ramanu themself is there, and they seem exasperated as they wave us over. "You know, when I told you to help, I didn't intend for you to bring Eve *here*."

"I know," Lenora says primly. "But I'm still helping. I'll keep her safe so you can focus on Azazel."

I know Ramanu called her a witch and that magic exists, but it's still hard to wrap my head around humans using it. Ramanu, on the other hand, looks visibly relieved. "Thanks, love." They press a quick kiss to her lips and nudge us backward into an open doorway. "Stay here."

A hush falls over the crowd as Brosh steps out of an alley and into the cleared space. He's still grinning as if he's not worried in the least. *I* would be less worried if he didn't seem so confident as he rolls his massive shoulders and bounces on his toes like a boxer ready to go. I'm pretty sure his claws are longer than they were in the castle too. The easier to disembowel the man I love with.

Azazel walks out of the castle a few moments later. He's changed into a pair of pants and little else. It seems like a terrible idea. Where is his armor? Shouldn't he have a damned helmet or something? At least a neck guard to keep from having his throat ripped out!

Brosh yanks his shirt over his head and tosses it to the ground. "The mighty Azazel. Ready to die, cousin?"

Azazel doesn't speak a word. He simply holds out a hand and crooks his fingers in a gesture that conveys "let's get this over with." I don't know if his lack of theater is comforting or concerning, just a mask for a deeper worry.

There's no time to decide. Brosh charges him, more bull than bargainer. He's so incredibly fast—too fast. Azazel jumps back but too late; a swipe of Brosh's claws opens up four deep gashes on Azazel's chest.

I slap my hands over my mouth to keep my cry of concern internal. I won't be the one to distract him, not when he needs every bit of his wits about him.

"Very good," Lenora murmurs in my ear. "You're doing well, Eve."

Why be concerned about *me* when he may very well die right before my eyes?

There's no space to ask. Brosh is on the attack again, swinging wildly. Azazel barely dodges the swipes, barely keeps a step ahead of his cousin. They circle the cleared space, sweat already gleaming on their bare skin. Sweat and blood on Azazel's.

And Azazel hasn't landed a single hit.

I don't realize I've started shaking until Lenora wraps an arm around my shoulders. "Shh, shh, it's fine. He's playing a good game of strategy. I know it's hard to see when you care about the person involved—trust me, I know—but he's got things under control."

Her words buzz over me but don't penetrate. Not when my heart is being stalked by his enemy, his cousin, who clearly wants him dead. And he's slowing down. Brosh lands a kick to Azazel's chest and two swipes to his chest and shoulder. More blood paints the cobblestones. Only one person's blood.

Brosh laughs and spreads his arms. "Is this your leader? He's as weak as he's made our territory. Pathetic." He turns . . . and runs right into Azazel's claws.

I gasp. The sound is lost in the midst of the crowd doing the same thing. Someone screams. A handful of people cheer.

Azazel appears tormented as he holds his cousin's shoulder and shoves his claws deeper into Brosh's stomach. Deeper and up . . . to rip out his heart. The man falls to the ground, dark eyes glassy with death. Azazel stares at the bloody heart in his claws and drops it on top of Brosh's body.

As if sensing my gaze, he lifts his eyes to mine. There's nothing of the man I've come to know so well, of the bargainer I love, there. Only emptiness.

Ramanu steps forward and raises their voice enough to be heard over those gathered. "The challenge has been issued, accepted, and completed. Brosh is dead. Azazel is victorious!"

This time, the cheers are loud enough to shake the very city.

Lenora squeezes my shoulder. "That's about enough of that. Let's get out of here."

"Yeah," I say numbly. It's not even the death that's rocked me this time. It's the implication. Brosh is dead. Azazel managed to do it honorably, which removes the threat against me, once and for all. That means I can go back to my life. I can go home.

Too bad home has started to feel a whole lot like a magical castle and a giant bargainer who holds my heart.

CHAPTER 20

EVE

*A*zazel finds me in my room barely an hour later. He's taken the time to shower, which I both appreciate and resent. My emotions make no sense, not even to me, so I do my best to hold them in and wait for him to speak first.

He doesn't make me wait long. "I need you to sign this." He pulls a short stack of papers from his jacket and sets them on the table. A pen appears shortly after.

It's happening. The thing I wanted so desperately for so long. I didn't expect it to feel so hollow. "Just like that."

"I gave you my word, Eve." He keeps his tone carefully distant. As if I truly am just another contract to him. I know it's a lie, that it's just to protect himself, but it hurts more than I expect.

I don't even read the papers before I scrawl my name in the appropriate spot and toss the pen aside. "Are you happy?"

"Are you?"

I refuse to cry, no matter how my throat clenches or my eyes burn. But I can't meet his gaze either. "I don't know how to feel, Azazel." I swallow as best I can. "I'm glad you're okay."

"Brosh never had a chance of beating me," he says softly. "He doesn't have the experience or the patience. He was a fool to threaten you, and even more of a fool to come here to challenge me." He reaches out and brushes my hair back from my face. "But you're safe, so it was worth the cost."

I can't speak. I can't even *think*. "What now?"

"Now, I take you home."

I don't expect him to mean *right this second*, but the room swirls around me in a sickening way that I recognize from the night he brought me here. I open my mouth to tell him to wait, to just give me a moment, but everything goes dark before I can utter a single word.

* * *

I WAKE UP IN DARKNESS . . . except not true darkness. For the first time in months, I hear horns honking and the normal night sounds of the city. *My* city. I sit up so fast, my head spins. "Azazel!"

There's no answer. Why would there be? I'm back in my apartment with its cool-blue walls, thick carpet underfoot, and silly little treasures that I can't help but collect. Alone. I shiver. This space—*my* space—has never felt so barren before.

A vibrating sound makes me jump halfway out of my skin before I recognize my phone, lit up on my nightstand. Right. We have phones here. I fumble for it, the pressure in my chest loosening a fraction when I see Pope's name on the screen. "Pope?"

"Where the fuck have you been?" There's nothing of Pope's customary smooth tone in the question. In fact, they sound downright haggard. "It's been *days*, Eve. I get an SOS call from you, but when my guy gets into the hotel room, there's no one there. I've had my people searching high and low for you. I thought you were dead." Their voice breaks on the last word.

"I'm sorry." I press my free hand to my forehead. "It's, uh, a long story involving some light kidnapping."

"Light kidnapping." Their tone goes low and dangerous. "Is he there with you right now?"

"No," I whisper. "I don't think I'll ever see Azazel again." Somehow, during all the frustration and fury, it never felt real that Azazel would be removed from my life entirely.

I didn't even get to say goodbye.

Pope takes a deep breath, and when they speak again, they sound more like themselves. "I'm on my way. Do I need to bring a doctor with me?"

"No. I'm okay. Shaken up, but otherwise fine." Except for the gaping hole in my chest where my heart used to be.

Pope doesn't believe me, and I don't blame them. When they walk into my apartment an hour later, I can actually *see* the toll of the last few days. It's there in their bloodshot dark-brown eyes, in the way their normally lustrous medium-brown skin has gone waxy. Their locs are pulled up away from their face, but even those don't have as much bounce as I'm used to. Pope walks directly to me and pulls me into a hug that threatens to crush my ribs to dust. "I was so fucking worried about you."

"I know. I'm sorry. I didn't exactly have a choice."

They step back but grip my shoulders, as if they can't quite believe I'm here. That makes two of us. "Tell me everything."

And so I do. The truth. Pope watches me closely. There's no shock, no denial. Just a deep curiosity and investment in the story. Right up until the moment I explain how I got home.

They sit back and shake their head. "He's a fool."

"He did what I wanted."

"Except it's *not* what you wanted." They roll their eyes. "You've wanted two things from the moment I've met you, Eve. Freedom and to be someone's first priority. Not too much to ask in the grand scheme of things. All he had to do was talk to you and I'm sure you could have figured something out." They shake their head. "I'm glad you're home. I was losing my mind with worry. But it's clear you're not staying long."

I blink. "You're making a lot of assumptions."

"Am I?" Pope smiles. "You forget. I know people, and I know *you* especially." They reach out and clasp my hand. "I'll be sad to see you go. Promise to check in periodically and let me know you're alive."

The room feels strangely liquid around me in a way that has nothing to do with magic and everything to do with shock. "You're such an asshole. You couldn't even give me a few minutes to figure it out on my own."

"Time is money, baby." They squeeze my hand and rise, stretching their arms over their head and making something in their spine pop. Their expression goes soft. "Unless you really mean to pick up your life right where you left off as if the last couple months didn't happen and you aren't in love with Azazel."

I grit my teeth even as my chest flutters alarmingly. "I happen to like my life."

"You were content. Not happy." They shrug at my shock. "You're one of my best friends, Eve. I wouldn't have let you continue with the work if it was hurting you. You enjoyed yourself, but from the moment you started, you were simply killing time."

"Stop analyzing me," I snarl. "It's rude."

"It's what I do, and you love me for it." They slip their phone from the pocket of their tailored pants. "Now, do you want to take a few days for your pride to heal from the mortal wound of my knowing you well enough to predict your next move . . . or do you want to summon your demon lover?"

I narrow my eyes. "You're taking the idea of demons and other realms too well. You didn't even ask me if I was on drugs."

"More things in heaven and earth and all that." They wave it away. "I move in a lot of strange circles, and some of them are less human than you'd imagine."

I can't even process what they're saying right now. Obviously I'm aware that Lenora came from this realm and she's a witch with magic of her own so that means there must be other magic here . . . but I didn't expect it to intersect my life. "Why didn't you tell me?"

They shrug. "Some things are best kept separate; you never showed any interest in the paranormal. It's not the sort of thing you bring up in mixed company unless you want to get those wild-eyed looks that I deeply dislike. Little did I know one of your favorite clients was a demon."

This is all happening too fast . . . and yet not fast enough. It's so easy to get swept up in Pope's energy. Sometimes I dig my heels in out of sheer habit, but the truth is that they're right. I already made my decision.

I inhale deeply and try to think. "I need a lawyer too."

Pope's brows wing up. "A lawyer."

"One specializing in contracts." The plan snaps into place. I don't know how to summon a demon, but it can't be that hard, right? Especially if Pope knows people who are familiar with the concept. "Once I get that ironed out, it's time to summon Azazel."

And this time, it truly will be a lifetime contract.

CHAPTER 21

AZAZEL

*A*side from that mess with Mina and her vampire lovers, no one has attempted to summon me in longer than I care to count. It takes me several long beats admit to understand what the gentle tugging in my chest means. Longer still to give in to the pull.

I have no interest in contracts and deals at the moment. In the days since I delivered Eve home, it's rapidly become clear that I've made a terrible mistake. Everything is *wrong*. The light is dimmer. Food tastes of nothing. Everyone is furious with me, from Ramanu to the damned castle. They don't understand.

If I hadn't taken her home the first moment I could, I never would have. I'm not proud of that realization. Letting the woman I love wither away to nothing, trapping her in a life away from everything she's ever known, welcoming her hate because at least that means she's feeling something for me . . . I would have done it.

That makes me a monster.

I endure Ramanu's spiked silence and Lenora's cutting remarks. I don't complain when the castle makes every trip four times as long as it needs to be. I even endure a strongly worded letter from Alice about how I've fucked up.

And now someone has the *audacity* to summon me. The tug in my chest becomes stronger, more insistent. They aren't giving up. I should kill them where they stand. I'm certainly in the mood for it. But when I materialize in the human realm, it's not a stranger outside the summoning circle.

It's Eve.

She's not alone. At her right, Pope lounges against the arm of her sofa, dressed in a suit with far too many buttons undone to be entirely decent. At her left, the witch responsible for the summoning, a white man with short blond hair and a world-weary expression. He sits back the moment I become corporeal. "Good luck."

"Thank you for your service. Your fee has already been deposited," Pope drawls. Their gaze rakes over me. "This is your true form? I have to say I prefer it."

It's only then that I realize my glamor hasn't taken hold. Maybe that's something to be concerned about, but I can't quite manage to focus on anything but *her*. Eve kneels just outside the circle. She's still wearing the same thing she was when I brought her home, loose pants and a tunic. Her hair is even the same, braided back from her face. "How long?"

"Less than twenty-four hours."

I look around the space. This must be Eve's apartment. I've never had cause to visit—some lines shouldn't be crossed, even for prospective bargains—but it feels like her. "What am I doing here, Eve? You have no reason to be dissatisfied with the terms of the nullification. I gave you enough money that you should never have to work again if you're not interested."

Pope hisses out a curse under their breath, and Eve looks at me like she wants to bludgeon me with something. She shakes her head. "You're a damned fool, Azazel." She reaches behind her and produces a single sheet of paper. "I want a new contract."

My racing thoughts slam to a standstill. "What?"

"New terms." She waves the paper at me. "Read it."

But I can't make my body move. "The only thing you wanted the entire time you were with me was to be free."

"Yes. Freedom." She waves the paper again. "That word has many meanings. Read it."

I carefully take the paper and scan it. I reach the end, and my confusion only blooms. I read it again. And then a third time. "What is this?" On the fourth time through, things start to click into place. "You're . . . proposing."

"Yes," Eve says primly. "You offered me a lifetime contract before. I want a new one—on equal footing."

The contract is simple enough as such things go. It's got similar terms to the one she signed all those nights ago, except it's designed to go both ways instead of my protecting her from harm. She wants to . . . protect me too. I reach the clause about children and I actually stop breathing. "You want kids."

"I want to keep the door open on the decision about whether or not to have children." When I manage to tear my gaze from the paper to her face, it's to find her blushing. She clears her throat. "It's something that should be discussed at length, but if I have your children, they will *not* be taken from me."

This can't be real. Surely this is a dream that I'll wake from at any moment. "But . . . why?"

Pope scoffs and leans down. "Good luck with this, darling. Remember to visit." They press a kiss to the top of her head and saunter off. A few seconds later, the sound of a door shutting announces their departure.

Eve rises unsteadily to her feet. "It's because I love you, Azazel."

Words I've desperately wanted to hear from her. Words I

know in my heart of hearts that I don't deserve. "But *why*? I've lied to you, kidnapped you, kept you trapped in my home for months."

"Yes," she agrees easily. "I'm not saying you weren't a high-handed asshole for doing all of that without talking to me first —*or* that I'll allow it going forward."

I feel like I'm lost at sea and have just sighted land but I can't trust the sight enough to be sure it's real. "Then why?"

"Because you're a good man." She takes a slow step forward, breaking the line of the summoning circle. "Because you've sacrificed and fought and done the hard work to help your people, even if there were those among them who didn't want the change. Because you want to share that prosperity instead of keeping it only for your territory." Another step and she's close enough to touch. I don't dare lift my hand. Eve smiles softly. "Because, even though it was the only option you had, you didn't want to kill Brosh."

I flinch. "It shouldn't have come to that."

"I know." She gently places her hands on my bare chest. "I won't pretend that things will be smooth sailing between us. You're overprotective and I'm fiercely independent. You'll try to make decisions for me and I'll shut you down the moment you do. You'll step back and allow me my freedom, even if it scares you. We'll figure it out. I have the utmost faith in that."

I can't stop myself from catching her hips and tugging her a little closer. "You have a life here. You have your work. And Pope."

"Yes," she says simply. "I'd like to visit Pope when it's feasible. But the rest? There's no shortage of work to be done in your territory." Her smile broadens. "Your sex workers don't have a guild like the other trades, even if they're not persecuted the way professionals are in this city. I'd like to create one for them."

She takes my breath away. "That will take time and a lot of effort."

"It's a good place to start."

I nod slowly. "You're right. It's a good place to start." I make myself release one hip to stare at the slightly crumpled contract again. "You really mean this, Eve? A marriage. A partnership. Potentially children?"

"I love you."

I shiver. "I'll never get tired of you saying those words. I may need to hear them a few hundred more times. Immediately."

She laughs, the sound pealing through the apartment. "Sign the contract, marry me, and you can hear them as often as you like."

I pull her with me as I move to the short table in front of her couch. There's a trio of pens there, as well as another stack of papers. "What's this?"

"Oh, I had to figure out what to do with my stuff and finances. I signed it all over to Pope with instructions on how to donate. Their notary was already here with the lawyer, so it will be done as soon as I'm gone."

She hasn't been home long enough to change her clothes, but she's managed all this? It seems to defy belief. I look into her dark eyes. "Are you sure?"

"Yes." Her brows pull together. "Are you? I realize that I just threw this at you and you may need some time to—" She watches me sign and smirks. "Guess not."

I take her hand and bring it to my lips. "Marry me, baby girl. Be my queen."

"You aren't a king. Technically."

I shrug. "Both things can be true at the same time. You may not—technically—be the territory's queen. But you'll be *my* queen."

Eve beams. "In that case, I accept. But you should know that I want a lavish wedding and will likely drive you bonkers in the planning."

I can't keep a goofy grin off my face as I rise and pull her into my arms. "Believe me when I say I literally cannot wait. I'll relish every moment." I kiss her. "I love you. Come home with me."

She smiles against my lips. "I love you. Take me home. Forever."

Made in the USA
Las Vegas, NV
26 December 2024